Pilgrims Into Light

By
Richard Lebherz

PublishAmerica
Baltimore

© 2003 by Richard T. Lebherz.

All rights reserved. No part of this book may be reproduced, stored in a retrieval system or transmitted in any form or by any means without the prior written permission of the publishers, except by a reviewer who may quote brief passages in a review to be printed in a newspaper, magazine or journal.

First printing

ISBN: 1-59286-289-6
PUBLISHED BY PUBLISHAMERICA, LLLP
www.publishamerica.com
Baltimore

Printed in the United States of America

For Louise and Denton Cooley

Best Wishes
Richard Ribley

*To love somebody is not just a strong feeling –
it is a decision, it is a judgment, it is a promise.*

– From *THE ART OF LOVING*
Eric Fromm

Chapter One

Michael Humphrey gazed intently up at the filmy white clouds that gamboled like fluffy ewes across the blueness of the sky. He turned his head earthward, noticing the cherry tree whose limbs were ladened with puffed buds that would soon burst open. Cheerful, noisy sparrows racketed in the dark. Heart-shaped green leaves of the ivy climbed tenaciously up towards the second-story windows. Crocus spotted the grass with dots of white and yellow stars. Against the house, hyacinth buds were tinged with a bruised blue tint. There was a warm promising breeze imprisoned in the branches of the lilac bushes, rattling as they were begging to be freed. Michael felt the tremendous lightness in the air, an almost carefree abandonment that came, he thought, with spring in Washington. Then his fretful eyes became more intent with thought.

Another spring, he acknowledged emptily, knowing full well that another spring had little meaning for him. Only, he had to admit, this year he wanted desperately for it to *have* a meaning. He was impatiently irritated particularly with himself because he knew he did not care, did not care about the clouds overhead, the cherry tree, or the cheerful sparrows. In fact, he knew he did not care about anything, least of all, about himself. He knew it. He had known it for some time now. I don't give a damn about being alive, he confessed. I wish the whole thing were over. He touched the handle of the cup he had been drinking his coffee from as if to make certain there *was* a reality outside himself. "It's true," he said aloud. "I really don't give a damn." Quickly he turned his head guiltily towards the house to see if his wife might have overheard. Fortunately no one was there.

"I'm going out in the garden with my coffee," he had said half an hour earlier. His wife had smiled considerately as if she understood his sudden need to be out in the spring-like weather. He had been reading his *Post* before then, when quite unexpectedly he had glanced out in the yard, noticing the irregular patches of sunlight on the grass. Somewhere off to the side was the incessant chirp of sparrows. Exactly at that moment a painful, twisting ache punched him in the pit of his stomach, forcing him to stand up unexpectedly, for he felt that if he did not go outside immediately, he would be ill. He knew what *that* ache meant. He had it many times before, only lately the attacks had become more frequent. The sensation simply meant that he wanted to get out of his house, away from his dull government job ... only that was as far as he ever seemed to get. Anywhere? Away to whom? To what? He never knew.

With deliberate slowness he had walked out into the garden because he was half afraid that if he hurried, showed too much enthusiasm for getting away, his wife would notice and suspect his behavior. She had the uncanny ability of being able to decipher these small meaningless actions that apparently denoted great significance. And he disliked her for it. Out there he had begun reading his paper again, at least he tried to, and in order to cover up any suspicion he took periodic sips from his cup, but as hard as he struggled to behave as if nothing were wrong, inside his thoughts were racing disturbingly about.

For over half an hour now he had been sitting there enjoying his thoughts and his perceptions, earnestly trying his best to *feel* something. Yet he was aware that there was nothing for him to feel nor had there ever been. His life had been flat since the day he was born. Now, if it were possible, it was even flatter than that. Life in Georgetown had acquired a gay futile monotony that was not exactly too difficult for him to adjust to. They had been living there for the past eight years. Their neighbors had generously and immediately accepted them into the community, for Mona had a very special way of making friends easily. Boisterous Senator Drake who lived next door had taken a great "shine" to Mona. Mrs. Drake had turned out to be a second mother to them all.

So, within a year or two they had fitted themselves with ease into the everyday life of Georgetown as if they had been living there since childhood. Automatically, they were taken up socially by the diplomatic set and under the benevolent eye of Mrs. Drake they had even begun to make great strides politically. He could still remember the evening after they had gotten home from one of The White House extravaganzas when Mona had said excitedly, "Darling, we're a frightful success." Her proclamation had chilled him to the very bone. In his own field, the agency he worked for kept raising his salary as if they were afraid he was going over to a competitive agency. Finally, he decided to attribute his lusty success to a basic indifference, which, he was certain, his colleagues mistook for casualness.

Then one day, two years ago, this flatness had ended for him. He had been sitting on one of the benches in Dumbarton Oaks watching the crisp red and yellow leaves falling listlessly to the ground, listening to their slight whisperings as they tapped other leaves in the falling, when out of nowhere he was overtaken by a strange uncomfortable feeling that somehow, in some way, he was no longer the person he had been. In some unexplained manner a *new* Michael Humphrey had succeeded the other, and was in fact sitting in the other's place. This new Michael Humphrey sat there trembling, for his hands shook dreadfully, and for the first time that the old one could recall, he actually noticed the new one's hands, noticed the shape, the size, the roundness of the flat nails, realizing with a shock that they were certainly *his* hands. They were real and they were a part of him. The sensation of this realness frightened him even more than the uncanny feeling that he was not the same person who had sat down there on the bench in the beginning.

For with this realness, this immediacy, had come a terrifying comprehension that he was alive, that he was real, that he was separate, or whatever else you might want to call it, and with this awareness came an overwhelming sense of fear that caused the old Michael Humphrey to jump up and hurry out of the park.

When he had gotten home, he rushed into the kitchen to make a drink. While he stood pouring a sizeable amount of whiskey into a glass, his wife had entered, taken one quick glance at his face and asked, "Is there something wrong, Michael?"

His hand trembled so that some of the whiskey spilled. "Wrong?" he had retorted miserably. "In what way?"

Then she had said the worst remark possible. "You don't seem like your old self somehow." The trembling glass he was holding smashed loudly to the floor.

Since that afternoon he had *not* been himself. He was *two* selves. One doing the everyday routine of living while the other watched patiently, never condemning, never nagging, waiting gratefully for an off moment when he would finally sit down by himself, then quietly he would be replaced by that calmer self, that wiser self, causing him to dislike the other everyday self that had gotten married, made money, lived in Georgetown, and went to all the proper parties in the evening. Much to his dismay, this other self was becoming stronger, reappearing more frequently, for certainly he realized that it had been this *other* self who had lured him out into the garden, out into the sunlight where spring had settled down lightly over everything.

"Darling?" came his wife's voice breaking through his thoughts. She was calling from one of the second story windows. "Would you mind walking down to Magruder's? I need some red wine for tomorrow. The Bracknells will be here. You'd better get some gin, too. I asked Ben and the Senator over for cocktails this evening." She paused a moment. "I asked your secretary and her husband over, too. I thought it would be a good time since they've been back from their honeymoon now for over a month."

"Oh no!" he shouted back irritably. "I see her five days a week at the office. Do I have to entertain her over the weekend too?"

His wife stared disconcertedly down into the garden. "I'm sorry, Michael. I didn't realize you felt that way. I can call her back and say–"

"No, don't do that," he said impatiently. He stood up. "Just let it go." He headed for the house. Once inside, he took his empty coffee cup out into the kitchen, sat it down, and as he walked back into the living room, he noticed that his wife was standing up at the head of the stairs watching him.

"Michael," she said, coming hurriedly down towards him. "I know it's not the best time to mention this but you've got to tell me what the matter is. We can't go on like this. We can't."

"What do you mean, what the matter is?" he repeated, as if she were making a mistake. "Nothing is the matter." He saw that confused, pained expression on her face, which aggravated him even more than her question. "Can't anyone around here have any privacy at all? Do we have to make every thought we have community property?" He watched her bite her lip while she tried stubbornly to hold back tears. He realized that he hurt her again; so gently he reached over to touch her shoulder. "I'm sorry, Mona. Please try to overlook it."

"I can overlook what you said," she replied reluctantly, "But I can't go on overlooking what you're doing to us."

Now Michael Humphrey was very proud of his wife. He recognized in her a vitality towards living that he envied. She was satisfied with the world she had made. She had fought for it with all the energy she possessed. Her strong, capable hands held on to life while her energetic eyes reached out for even more. She was going somewhere. He had nowhere to go. There were many times when he felt exactly like a little boy tagging behind in the wake of her purpose. She had a rudder to her existence. His boat was without a sail. And it was slowly sinking. He knew that she was more than right about a great many remarks she made concerning his selfish behavior, but he found himself unable to correct them. He glanced into her dark eyes, then pleasantly noted how carefully she had combed her jet black hair, parting it in the middle, and with his fingertip he touched the end of her slender nose, remembering how her nostrils trembled with pleasure whenever they made love. Her full lips were slightly parted as if she wanted to speak. "I'll go get the wine before I forget it," he said. Carefully he bent over to kiss her lightly on the cheek. "Be patient with me right now. Please."

She stepped back, looked into his eyes for a hidden meaning, then nodded her head resignedly. A smile trembled on her lips. "I'll try my best, Michael, but at times I don't think I can bear it too much longer."

"Thanks," he said. Turning, he whistled for the dog. Annette came bounding playfully down the steps and as he slipped the leash onto her collar she licked his hand affectionately.

"She adores you, you know."

He scratched the poodle behind the ear. "I think she does." He opened the door. "I might go for a walk before lunch," he said self-consciously. "Don't worry about me if I'm not back right away."

She nodded her head happily. "And don't forget to stop at Magruder's."

Just as he started out of the door, she panicked. "Michael?" she called out. As he turned, she touched the sleeve of his coat reverently and said proudly, "Remember, I love you." She turned quickly then fled up the stairs.

Michael stood there for a second or two, but when Annette pulled at the leash, he turned and closed the door behind him. Once outside he headed for Wisconsin Avenue.

Chapter Two

After Anna Martin had paid the taxi driver, she nervously picked up a small black suitcase, got out of the car, then closed the door as quietly as she could. The driver raced the motor, shook his head, then sped away, leaving her standing full of uncertainty in front of a large, old, yellow painted house with huge box bushes on each side of the steps. She stood there obviously indecisive about whether she should go in or flee down the sloping pavement. Her thin fingers curled tensely around the leather handle of the suitcase. Her haunted, deep set eyes glanced anxiously at each window as if she half expected to discover a face watching her mysteriously from behind one of the curtains.

Nervously she fingered her coat. Unexpectedly she made the sign of the cross. She was unaware that she had resorted to this gesture for she made it unconsciously, in a way naturally, but at the same time there was in it a repetition that robbed the gesture of its full significance. Feeling surer of herself, however, she stepped forward up the red-bricked walk, then full of embarrassment she lifted the polished brass knocker upward, letting it fall discreetly down against the door. She shrank from the sound, imagining it to be louder than it actually was. A Negro woman who she had never seen before opened the door immediately as if she had been behind it waiting for her knock.

"Good mawning," she said pleasantly. "Is you Miss Anna?" The Negro woman stepped respectfully aside to let her enter.

"You come right in," she said, reaching out for Anna's suitcase, which she relinquished reluctantly. Carefully the maid placed it over by the table in the hallway. "Your grandmother told me to tell you she was just finishing up her letter writing. She'll be down directly."

"Shall I wait in here?" Anna asked, nodding her head towards the front parlor.

"In there will be fine, Miss Anna," said the maid, smiling affectionately at her. Then she noticed Anna's coat. "Why don't you let me take your coat?"

Anna hesitated. "I guess it would be best." Shyly she began unbuttoning each button carefully, and turning aside she slipped out of it. She stood there wearing a plain black woolen dress cuffed and collared in white. There were no buttons on it for they were hidden underneath a strip of material that ran down the entire length of the dress. The collar itself was unusually high and fitted modestly about her neck. She glanced over at the maid to see if she noticed anything unusual.

But the maid seemed not to notice her embarrassment because she had reached out for the coat. "You just go in there and make yourself to home."

Anna smiled her thanks, paused on the threshold of the parlor, then stepped slowly inside. She stopped still, a thin smile impressed itself on her lips. Her eyes closed for a second. In her ears she could hear the familiar, dutiful ticking coming from the clock on the mantle, the clock with the small enameled roses scattered around its face. In the far corner came the hissing sound of steam singing in the radiator. She opened her eyes quickly. They found the blue bowl of forced lily-of-the-valley sitting on the table. There were settees on each side of the table where Anna could remember sitting while her grandmother sat across from her and her brother reading Grimm's Fairy Tales in her rich, vibrant voice. Yes, thought Anna gratefully, there is permanence here, too, in every piece of beautiful upholstered furniture, in the fading but regal portraits of her ancestors on the wall, in the very precise way in which each object was placed on the shiny, well-polished tables. She was familiar with this kind of permanence. In the Convent where she had just come from it was in the sitting rooms where heavy oak chairs and tables sat about, in the crucifix, in the endless statues that lined the corridors.

Over the marble mantle was a large square mirror. Up the sides, plump golden cupids played. Slowly, as if hypnotized, Anna walked towards the reflected image of herself, scrutinizing it longingly for she had not studied herself closely for over a year. She stopped directly in front of the mirror, facing herself squarely. Her sensitive hands reached up to touch her short-cropped hair, cropped short enough to make her resemble a youth, cropped short enough to obliterate her sex, leaving only a thin face, colorless cheeks, pale lips pressed tensely together, but it was into her own eyes that she gazed rudely, seeking an answer that the reflected image refused to give. Her hands moved downward while the fingers trembled and touched her sharp chin. Tears sprang up, rimming her eyes enough to make her reflection impossible to see. Her lips quivered, her hands were clenched so tightly that the color left them. For one wild, uncontrollable moment she wanted to fling herself onto one of the settees and cry. She had been in control of herself long enough. She had earned this lessening of tension, but just as she was about to move towards the settee, she saw in the mirror the reflection of her grandmother's towering figure watching her from the doorway. Anna turned about as if she had been caught at petty theft, but her grandmother's warm smile made her feel foolish and stupid.

"My dear Anna," she said, crossing the room with her arms outstretched. "How nice of you to come to me like this." She enfolded her granddaughter benevolently within her embrace and patted her head thinking she was still quite young instead of almost twenty. "We shall have a splendid time together before you return to your parents. I can't tell you how good it is to see you like this." She held her away slightly for she wanted to get a more complete picture of her granddaughter, her sharp blue eyes wanted to take inventory of what was perhaps missing, and what might have surreptitiously been counted in. Anna's eyes were pierced with what she took to be despair, and deeply ringed from obvious countless nights of no sleep whatsoever, turning and tossing in an uncomfortable bed with her great inner problem, now over, and coming up or back into the light once more. Mrs. Ross touched her granddaughter's pale cheeks, shook her head sadly, then said, "Did they never ever let you see the sun?"

Anna backed away full of embarrassment. "Yes, I saw the sun," she defended them quickly, only she felt the urge to add, *But not the Son.*

"Come," said her grandmother with great authority. "Do let's sit down her for a moment. I've asked Mary to bring us tea directly." She noticed consternation on her granddaughter's face. "Mary hasn't been with me very long," she explained.

Anna watched her grandmother as she sat down majestically across from her, carefully fluffing up her white lace collar and smoothing her purple dress around her legs. Pinned, as always, on her right shoulder was a nosegay of – this time – violets, freshly picked, and held in place by a diamond clip. Her grandmother's hair was silvery white billowing regally up in soft puffs. When she was much younger, Anna had secretly believed that her grandmother actually wore a wig, the kind Marie Antoinette instigated at Court, because her hair was so remarkably neat with never one strand of it askew or a hairpin showing.

"Come," said her grandmother, patting the settee. "Do sit down. You must be quite tired coming all that way by bus. I wish you had let me send for you as I suggested. You really should have let me, you know. It could not have been at all comfortable riding like that after all you've been through." She realized she had mentioned *it* after all, which caused her to falter, then look pleadingly over at Anna for help, which, thank goodness she had decided to give.

Tense and awkward, Anna stepped around from behind the settee, sat down directly across from her grandmother, sat down carefully but precariously on the very edge of it with her back straight up and her moist eyes focusing deliberately on the oriental rug at her feet. "Grandmother," she said in a hollow, faded voice. "Are you terribly disappointed in me?" The moist, lifeless eyes looked up at last. "Because I've disappointed everyone." A dreadful sense of failure had taken possession of her completely.

She is wrung out, thought Mrs. Ross accurately, like a dish cloth. "Anna, no," she said, protesting even more than before. She disliked having people judge themselves because they never could see all the facts, all the evidence both for and against. "You must not think of what others are feeling at a time like this. You must be completely selfish and think only of yourself. Think only of what you feel towards yourself."

"I feel nothing," cried out Anna unexpectedly. "Nothing. There is no more feeling left inside me. Nothing, no. Only a tremendous silence."

Mrs. Ross was quite perplexed and made anxious by this quick, personal turn of events in the conversation. She certainly had prepared herself for some sort of situation, for after all, she was the first "outsider" that her granddaughter had to talk with, but she was at a loss of exactly how to deal with it. If the matter had been political, or social, her task would have been easier, but how does one discuss matters of the soul with another? How does one bring up God without feeling inadequate? "Anna," she said, leaning forward, "you must help yourself now. You must heal your own wounds. You are not the first young woman who has entered the religious life and found that she did not belong there. Why, I can understand perfectly," she said, almost rising from the settee in acclamation.

But Anna refused to accept her consolation. She had been hurt, her pride had been trampled under by a harsh reality, so she desired nothing better than to hurt someone else in return. "What is it you understand perfectly, Grandmother?" she asked derisively. "What *exactly* is it that you understand?"

Her grandmother stared in hurt surprise for she was instantly aware of her granddaughter's attempt to wound. Her mouth opened and closed as if unhinged momentarily, for she was trying to think of an adequate reply to make.

"Do you know exactly what it is to say good-bye to your family and friends, to say openly to the whole world that you are going to give yourself up to Christ, only…." she faltered, "…only to find out later that Christ doesn't want you?"

"My dear," said her grandmother softly, "you must stop tormenting yourself like this. You mustn't."

But Anna dug into her pain deeper and deeper. "Do you know exactly what it is to leave one world forever, to give it up willingly, then to find a home in another only that wonderful world is not for you, that Peace is not your Peace, that Love is not your Love?" Here she broke down sobbing, throwing up her hand in front of her face.

Staggered and upset by her granddaughter's sudden hysterics, Mrs. Ross tried desperately to think of some way to help. She wanted to say something wise, to do something to alleviate the obvious pain Anna was in, only she refrained prudently. There was nothing to do. One waited. One was there just in case.

As the tears surged and poured forth, cleansing and loosening up the tensions she could no longer bear to hold in, Anna felt a tremendous pressure lessening inside her head, as if all the nights of tossing on her bed in the convent hoping to solve her predicament had finally caught up with her. She began to experience a pleasure that she had not known for a long time, the luxury of feeling. Apparently, she decided, the realization that she did not have a religious vocation had sent her into a state of shock; for the time spent in the convent had made her aware that not only did she not have such a vocation, but that she had fabricated the one she thought she possessed. But day after day she deliberately refused to face up to this fact. She had romanticized her vocation, stubbornly held on to her particular version because she was afraid to let go and find herself another. In the end she had come to realize that a religious vocation is very much like the earth, firm and real.

What Anna had been preserving was the intimate glow of candles, the fragrant smell of incense, the silence and the darkness that let her share herself in romantic prayers with Jesus Christ. She had laid down her trembling life at His feet, as she thought an obedient bride should, offered herself up as an offering, submissive, pliant, vibrant as the strings of a harp, only no fingers reached out to play a tune. There was no response whatever. There was no sign of acceptance or rejection. There was only more silence and soft murmur of nun's voices praying in the background. "I *expect* nothing," she had cried out humbly in prayer, when in fact she had *hoped* for everything. As the weeks passed, her vocation crumbled apart gradually into what it was, a protection, an illusion that she no longer could maintain. What she had longed for, ached for in the beginning was to submit, to bow low before Christ, now she saw it for what it was and where her need had come from. One morning as she was kneeling in prayer, the truth of her situation came upon her. Very quietly she had fainted. The death of an illusion.

After that, Anna was besieged with bitter resentments. She resented herself, Christ, the convent, the nuns, but most of all herself. These tears were helping all of that now. Gradually the pain in her head subsided as well as her tears. Across the way in a blurry, watery mass sat her grandmother patiently waiting. Anna dried her eyes and blew her nose self-consciously. Finally she sat up straight, tried to smile feebly at her grandmother, and between gulps for air she managed to say, "I'm sorry. I didn't mean to."

"There now," said her grandmother gently. Reaching over, she picked up a silver bell from the table and rang it. (She did not notice the stricken expression that came on Anna's face at the sound of it, for the bell looked exactly like the one used in the convent at communion time to announce the coming of Jesus Christ.) "Mary must have forgotten about tea," went on Mrs. Ross. "She's only been with me now for a little over six months. Do you remember the first time you and David came down to visit me when you were, what was it, six or seven?"

"Six," smiled Anna.

"You didn't like it here very much then, did you? I hope you do now?" She reached impulsively across the table to pat her granddaughter's hand. "Don't be afraid of me, Anna. I couldn't bear it if you were. I don't like fighting with people, you know. You understand, my dear, what I mean?"

"Yes, I understand," said Anna, wiping away the remainder of her tears.

"You can have a very happy visit with me. You've come at such a lovely time. Washington is never more beautiful than it is now. Spring just, well, baptizes everything so to speak, into something else. All my tulip bulbs are pushing up. In fact, dear, after tea I think it would do you a world of good to trot out for a short walk. You know where Dumbarton Oaks is, just up the hill. Go there. Sun yourself. Enjoy what's around you." She glanced impatiently out into the hallway. "I wonder where that girl can be? Sometimes she's dreadfully slow." Then she saw the maid making her way towards them with a large silver tray in her hands. "There she is. Anna, this is Mary Chase."

Mary smiled broadly, sitting the tray carefully down on the table. Anna liked her a little better this time. She wasn't as afraid of her as she had been at the door. There was a certain happy look about her eyes that attracted Anna. Then, too, Mary apparently knew nothing about her or where she had come from. In many ways the not knowing made the situation easier for Anna.

"Lemon or cream, dear," asked Mrs. Ross, holding up a cupful of steaming tea.

"Cream please." She took the cup and held it unsteadily in her hands. On a small plate there were several of the wafer cookies that they always had whenever there was tea. For the first time in a good many weeks Anna knew that she was beginning to feel happy again. She enjoyed this tremor of contentment. Her ordeal was now over and done with. Her tremendous burden had been let down. Quickly she reached for a cookie. "I remember these."

"I thought maybe you would," replied her grandmother happily. "Now let's drink up our tea so that you can go for a walk. We have lunch at one. That should give you plenty of time to enjoy Georgetown."

Anna bit into the cookie, took a deep swallow of tea. "You know, I haven't been out by myself now for over a year." She added humorously, "I may even be afraid."

Well now, thought Mrs. Ross to herself, that's better. A smile on her lips. A joke. "Have another?" She offered her the plate.

Suddenly a deep sigh escaped Anna's lips. Whether it was a sigh of relief or regret her grandmother could not tell.

Chapter Three

Michael Humphrey strolled leisurely along one of the many graveled paths of Dumbarton Oaks. Every now and again he would stop abruptly, listening to the sound of spring; bees humming nervously in the air, robins calling busily from tree to bush as they hectically constructed their nests. Once he held out his hand to the bold sunshine, feeling a tingling sensation on his skin from the naked heat. Impulsively, he bent down, then let Annette off the leash. He had never done this before. He always kept her under his control, but today he could not restrain himself. She tore away like a frisky black lamb, tearing around the grass in circles as if sudden freedom had gone straight to her head. He laughed sympathetically at Annette's gyrations because, for a change, he could appreciate Annette's behavior.

However, fifteen minutes later he began realizing that the dog had not reappeared. Angrily he whistled. No Annette. He whistled again, walking impatiently along the path. No obedient scurrying in the bushes. "Damn that dog," he said under his breath. "Why in hell did I let her off the leash?" He hurried up one path then down another. Suddenly he stopped still. He saw the dog. She was lying beside a young woman who was sitting on the grass. Annette was lying playfully beside her, readying to spring up in either direction if he came any closer.

"Annette," he called sharply. The poodle looked up in recognition but refused to move.

"I'll hold her for you," the young woman said as he came closer. "She's a very bright poodle."

As he bent down to get hold of the collar he said apologetically, "I hope she hasn't been annoying you."

"Oh, no," she assured him. "She's been amusing me with her tricks." She reached over affectionately to scratch one of Annette's silky clipped ears. "You don't know what it means to see a dog again."

There was something nostalgic about the way she said that which made him notice her purposely more than before. Could she have been sick? he wondered. In a hospital? Her skin was pale. She was thin and her eyes…. But there he stopped. Her eyes were arresting. They were large dark eyes, with long lashes that curled naturally at the ends. Her nose was firm. Her chin nicely shaped. Her hair, however, was cut unusually short, making her resemble a young Saint Joan, but above everything else she gave him the impression that there was a tragic sweetness in her character, a tragic compliance towards life.

"Where have you been?" he asked casually.

The young woman looked up quickly, a blush appeared on her cheeks. Suppose, she thought humorously, that I told him. What effect would it have on a perfect stranger? Would he be interested? Shocked? "I've been away," she said finally. "But I've just arrived here in Georgetown. I'm visiting my grandmother for a few weeks." Anna Martin studied his face timidly at first. She realized that he was one of the most handsome men she had ever seen. His dark black hair was flecked with white around his ears, which made him look most distinguished. His dark eyebrows and rich brown eyes made his full lips redder by contrast. "Do you live in Georgetown?" she asked, watching how the sunlight reflected on his face until he had to change his position.

Her question startled him, because for just a second he had an irrational desire to say that he did not, that he lived somewhere else, that in fact, he was not even from Washington. Instead, he replied matter of factly, "Yes, I do." The urgency that he had felt to be someone other than himself flicked out of consciousness. "Did you say that you had just arrived here?" he asked, giving her a friendly smile.

Even though there was a smile on his lips, when Anna glanced into his eyes she saw only a weary, bored look, for she was unusually sensitive to other people, so she was aware intuitively that here was a person who was as deeply troubled within as she had been these past few weeks. She wondered if there was anything she might do to help. In the convent she was used to simple, direct, uncomplicated relationships with nuns and novices. She was not certain he would appreciate her directness. She could tell his guard was up. His sense of competition was still strong. His pride was vast and personal. However, on an impulse, she asked sympathetically, "You're upset about something, aren't you?" She smiled knowingly. "Is there something I could do to help you?"

"Something you could do to help me?" he repeated incredulously, for she had caught him off guard. "Why," he laughed, "I was just about to ask you the same thing. You look like you just lost your best friend."

"Really," she said, still smiling. "In a way I have."

Then embarrassment set in. He reached out to rearrange Annette's leash. Anna stared blankly down at the grass. Finally he said cautiously, "What makes you think that *I* need help?" He perused her face with his fearful, fretful eyes.

"Something does," she replied hesitantly. She had begun to realize that perhaps she had gone too far. She had confronted his privacy with her indelicate prying, a problem she realized she would have to overcome. Up until recently she had always believed that honesty would cut through so much meaningless chatter as far as human relationships were concerned. Now she was just beginning to understand that with some people there was no short cut to a relationship. She would have to play the game closely, waiting for the proper move, the proper gesture, the proper word. Honesty apparently had no part in this type of tournament. If lucky, she supposed, honesty would be the prize in the end.

"What does?" he insisted.

She glanced directly into his eyes now, eyes full of disturbance, and yes, a kind of agony. She was determined not to go too far. His eyes were far too appealing. His gaze made her uncomfortable.

"What does?" he asked once more.

"There's just something about you," she began, feeling more uncomfortable as she went on. "About the way you look, the way you speak, that makes me feel you might need help of some kind."

What exactly was it about her that interested him? Why was there such a difference about her? She seemed to understand him in a way he had not understood himself. "And you might know *all* about that kind of need?" he asked quietly.

She hesitated. Did she? Reluctantly she nodded her head. "I might," she replied earnestly. "It's not an apparent need exactly, is it? I mean not like needing an umbrella when it rains. It's more of a yearning for something inside which you just don't quite ever seem to understand. You try to understand it. First you try one thing and then another. It's not this, not that, until you begin to narrow down, corner it somehow, then you reach for it, only...." she stopped pathetically.

"Only what?" he encouraged.

Her eyes filled with sudden tears. "Only it disappears between your fingers. Like an elusive ghost. Like a fragrance in the air." She had thought she had gotten over her experience but she knew now that she had not. The memory of her lost vocation pained her still.

He misunderstood her tears completely. Now he believed

earnestly that he understood what had caused her paleness, her thinness and the sorrow in her eyes. "Are you getting over a love affair?" he asked sympathetically.

Inside, for a moment, Anna reacted as if he had struck her full force but outside she remained calm, her eyes slowly turning to his. What a vastness separated people. Just the two of them sitting there were from worlds apart. Maybe, she thought, maybe it's just our inner pain that has made us sympathetic, brought us for the moment closer, and dares us to talk on. She had to tell him the truth now. There was no point in letting his thoughts stray down the wrong path. "I just got out of a convent," she said in a hollow, lifeless voice. "I was hoping to become a nun but I found out that I did not have the temperament nor the emotional qualifications necessary. I don't know if you could call that a love affair. Yet perhaps it was."

He stared at her completely perplexed. Her unusual confession shocked him. Confusion spread across his features. She's just trying to be dramatic, he thought. Yet, the paleness, the thinness, the short-cropped hair, the black dress. The odd expression in her very lovely eyes. Could she be telling the truth? He had never known anyone who had been in the religious life. He was not a Catholic himself. The whole world of religion was one he had never explored. Nor did he want to. Yet, here sat a woman who had tried but failed. He had a kind of admiration for her. She had felt an emotion deep enough to cause her to enter a convent. "I just can't believe it," he said, watching her face carefully. Suddenly he felt as if there were a hundred different questions he wanted to ask her about her feeling, about her belief.

"What's the matter?" she asked finally. She could not stand to see him watching her with such awesome curiosity.

"I don't know exactly," he admitted. "There's no reason in the world for me to doubt you but...."

"But what?" she asked, puzzled by his peculiar reaction.

"Oh," he said laughingly, "I've behaved this way many times before."

"You mean not wanting to believe what someone says?"

"Yes," he replied boyishly. "I have a dreadful habit of twisting things around to suit myself." He thought of his wife. "Some people say I don't face reality. They may be right. Then again, they might be wrong."

Reality, Anna thought. The word that meant so many different things to so many different people. "I've never known what reality is," she admitted honestly.

"I don't either," he agreed. "But there are times when I can tell I'm rearranging it. Like now. About you."

"But why don't you want to believe me?" she asked, completely mystified by his attitude.

He shook his head. "I never know the *why* about anything until it's too late. I can remember the first time I was actually conscious of not wanting to believe what actually was."

"When was that?" she asked.

He smiled. "Are you interested really?"

"Yes." She smiled back. You'd think we knew each other for years instead of minutes, she thought. "I'd like to hear."

Annette snuggled up against him. He reached down to pat her. "Well," he began, wondering why he wanted to tell her in the first place. "I guess I must have been around twelve. Usually every summer the family went up to a resort in Maine right on the coast. We lived in a large house not far from the water and every morning I used to get up before anyone else did and go out for my 'constitutional' as my mother called it. I would go out and walk along the beach, sometimes barefoot if the water wasn't too cold, then I would hunt for different-shaped shells that the morning tide had washed up from the night before." He stopped suddenly because he realized how unusual it was for him to be telling a perfect stranger this very personal account of his life. (Had he ever told it to Mona?) Yet, he realized that in lots of ways it was much easier to talk with a stranger because you did not know how they actually felt or would react about anything. "Every day I would follow this routine, except when it rained, until one morning as I was walking along the beach I saw something else that had been washed up by the tide. I went closer. A man's body was lying on its back, swollen and bluish in color. His eyes were covered with a whitish substance that frightened me most of all. I remember how I kept saying to myself that the man was *not* there at all. I did *not* believe that I was seeing it. I backed away and fled to my breakfast." His eyes became intense as if he were seeing the body all over again. "I was at first unable to eat but then I found I had to take myself in hand. I reasoned that if I could not eat, it was because I *had* seen a dead man's body lying out there on the beach. Since I had *not* seen it, I should be able to eat. So, I forced myself to eat every bit of that breakfast. You see," he glanced over at her, "I was training myself like a Spartan to ignore reality. Within a half an hour someone found the body. I never went near it. I never even told anyone I had seen it. 'But you must have seen it on your walk,' insisted my father. But I denied that I had. I suppose that I've been using that system ever since. When I see what I don't want to see, I ignore it. When I don't want to believe something that I know I believe, I can do that too. And for some reason which I don't quite understand at the moment, I do *not* want to believe that you've just come from a convent." He seemed puzzled by the implication. "Why do you think I behave that way?"

"I don't know," she said softly. "Perhaps it would be best then if we talked of something else." She could see that he was becoming quite upset and his conversation was beginning to make her uneasy.

Her suggestion to change the conversation seemed to snap him out of his preoccupation. He was aware of Annette stretched out on the grass, of the warmth in the air, of himself sitting and of the young woman with such interesting eyes. "Didn't you say," he began politely for the third time, "that you had just arrived in Georgetown?" She nodded her head. "Do you like it?"

"Very much," she said enthusiastically. "I used to come here to visit my grandmother when I was quite young. Georgetown always makes me feel like a different person. Everything is old. I like old things. I feel safer somehow with old things."

"Safer?" he questioned.

She smiled timidly. "When I'm inside my grandmother's old home, surrounded by antique chairs and beautiful old clocks, I feel that everything there is friendly. Do you know what I mean?" She studied his expression to see if he did.

"Maybe a little," he admitted, feeling for the moment that he, too, at times had felt this same safeness with the past. He had always felt, God knows, that he was at a loss in understanding the quick, fast-paced world he was enmeshed in. "Maybe there's more romance in the past too?" he suggested.

"Yes, and then too," she reached down for a piece of grass, "the past is *over*. It can't harm us again like it did. The present can, of course. The present is very *dangerous*."

"But what if the past should begin to catch up with you? What then?"

So that was his problem, she thought. "Perhaps you should let it," she hinted. "Then maybe you won't be afraid of it anymore. You will understand it."

"Will I?" he remarked apprehensively. He shook his head. "You know, I still can't believe you just came out of a convent. You don't really seem to belong in one."

"Apparently not," she said quickly, then glanced away.

He realized at once that he had unintentionally hurt her. "I didn't mean it the way it sounded," he said apologetically. "I think the convent lost a great deal when they let you go." There was such openness, such honesty in her face that he never felt uncertain or insecure. Her face was an open invitation for sympathy. "What was it like?" he asked, hoping he did not sound too inquisitive.

"The convent?"

"Yes, the convent," he said.

Now why did he want to know that? she wondered. Was he just being polite or was he naturally curious about such things? "Well," she began, not really wanting to, "I suppose most of all there was a feeling of...." She stopped for the best word. "A feeling of safeness there. I don't think I can explain it exactly, but in a world where there is little continuity, little ritual, well, a convent offers both. There is a rigorous pattern of activity set up which begins at four-thirty in the morning and continues right up until night time. Time is never wasted. You either become a part of these procedures or...." she hesitated embarrassingly, "...or you're winnowed out."

"But you're absolutely certain you felt safe there?" he asked, as if he were a physician seeking information from a patient.

"Yes," she said with certainty. "I did anyway."

"Exactly how does this safeness feel?" he went on with his questioning. Unconsciously he was on the track of something, but as usual he did not know what.

She had never seen anyone quite so interested in religious matters. "Like you have been raised up or separated from the world," she explained carefully. "You have been saved from it. You have become enclosed from it. You are protected from it. The very direction you are going in is the exact opposite of the world's. Your aims separate you but the convent seeks to protect those aims."

"How do you feel now sitting out here on the grass with the sun overhead?"

"You mean without the convent to protect me?" she asked. She paused to consider her feeling. "I guess if I were honest I would have to admit that until you came I was feeling forsaken in a way. Left out."

Yes, he could see that. Her vulnerability stood out, her defenselessness, her uncertainty, all of it was there on her face. "Did you have to leave?"

"Yes, I had to," she replied nervously.

"Did they make you?" he went on.

"*Make* me?" she replied. "Of course not. They didn't make me enter it." She began shaking the grass from her skirt.

"I hope I haven't embarrassed you," he said. "I mean about asking you so many questions."

She stood up. "Not really. But I think I have to be going now. My grandmother's waiting for me."

"Of course," he remarked. They both stood there for a second or two full of embarrassment. "May I walk you home?" he asked finally.

"I'd rather you didn't," she replied. Before he could say any more she had turned and walked away.

"Well, I'll be damned," he said aloud. He stood there for at least five minutes. He kept looking down at the grass where the impression of her body remained. He had never met anyone quite like her before. He was suddenly exceedingly curious about her, about her whole life, about her feelings. He realized with regret that he did not even know her name. Who was her grandmother? Where did she live? He felt he had to see her again. There was so much he wanted to ask. So much suddenly. Annette pulled impatiently at the leash. Reluctantly he started back. He kept hoping to see her but she was nowhere in sight.

He hardly entered the living room before his wife cried out, "You didn't get the wine!" He stood there empty-handed.

"Wine?" he said vaguely. Then he remembered. "Damn it, Mona, I forgot. I'll go right back and get it now. Red wine, wasn't it? And some gin." This time he left Annette behind because he could walk faster, but again, she was nowhere in sight.

Chapter Four

He realized, all of a sudden, that he had had far too many Old-Fashions, for the conversation seemed to be getting further away from his comprehension. He was rapidly sinking into that I-don't-give-a-damn attitude of his, which meant that he wanted only to divorce himself from the immediate surroundings, from the incessant voices saying meaningless things to one another, so he decided wisely not to have another. He sat his empty glass back down on the bar. When he turned around, he saw that the Senator was still trying to make a terrific impression on his secretary, Alice Grant. She was politely listening, while at the same time she nervously darted a look in the direction of her new husband, Hank Jidosky, who sat smouldering resentfully in the corner. He was rattling the ice in his glass noisily, evidently his manner of saying that he needed a refill, thought Michael. Isn't it odd how medical students seem to have an uncanny ability for attracting young, money-making girls who ultimately get them through medical school. Perhaps Alice had considered her husband a wise investment for the future. But he had thought Alice was a much smarter girl than that.

Suddenly Beatrice Drake laughed unusually loud. He turned his attention on her now. The Senator's wife was talking animatedly to Mona while the diamonds on her hands and wrist sparkled beautifully, giving off that pure, bluish, cold glint that Mona had told him was the difference between the real and the imitation. Michael knew her well enough after living next door for eight years that Bea was not pleased with the way things were happening on the couch across the way. He could tell by the furious way she sat with her back turned conspicuously away from the Senator that she was becoming agitated. When she pushed her cigarette out, as if it were the Senator instead, he knew that the Senator was in for it later.

The medical student rattled his glass again. Yes, thought Michael with amusement, the boy was getting more jealous too by the minute. He had now begun staring resentfully at the ice in his glass. He was obviously very uncomfortable. Just the way he slouched down in the chair showed he was. The way he had carelessly tied his tie suggested undoubtedly that he disliked being there. In fact, Michael was pretty certain Alice had probably had a great deal of trouble in getting him to come in the first place. He would look much more comfortable, thought Michael imaginatively, if he were sitting in front of a kitchen table covered with empty beer cans and uneaten sandwiches that Alice had most probably gone out and bought for his enjoyment. He could visualize Alive giving him all the stock arguments on why they had to go to the Humphreys for cocktails. After all, Mr. Humphrey was her boss. Didn't he want to improve himself? Get to know the right people? Especially people with a good income and a reputation in the social world? Doesn't a doctor have to start building up his practice long before he ever hangs out his shingle? Michael felt genuinely sorry for him. He walked over and asked if he would like another drink. After he had filled it with a big shot of bourbon, he handed it back to the student. Then impulsively he asked, "Would you care to see our garden?"

The relieved expression on the young man's face looked like he was being pardoned at the last moment for a crime he hadn't committed. He jumped up excitedly, spilling part of his drink on his suit.

"It's not a very large garden," went on Michael, ignoring the student's confusion, for suddenly he could see that the boy did not know if he should take his highball with him or leave it behind on the table. Evidently he decided that a drink in hand is worth two on the table because he held on to it and followed Michael out of the room. "Well, at least there's fresh air out here."

"Yes, sir," remarked the student apologetically, as if he had been in a way responsible for the fresh air.

"It certainly has gotten considerably cooler since this afternoon," remarked Michael, remembering how warm it had been on his walk in Dumbarton Oaks.

"Yes, sir," echoed the student. "Much cooler." He was remembering the afternoon he and Alice had spent in bed together. They had kicked the sheets off because of the heat.

The two men stood there awkwardly, momentarily untalkative, for this unexpected intimacy made them both self-conscious. In order to break the silence that was becoming more apparent, a silence that made the student automatically uneasy, he said nervously, "This is a nice place you got here, Mr. Humphrey." He hesitated for a second, then remarked wistfully, "Maybe one of these days Alice and me can live in a place like this. I think we'd be pretty happy."

Michael was quite surprised to realize that what was meaningless to him could very well be fulfillment to another. If he had known the boy more intimately he would have ventured to explain that even though you could have a place like this, the having of it would not necessarily bring you happiness. There were apparently other factors involved in personal happiness of which he was only just beginning to get a glimpse himself. "I hope you do get a place like this," he said sincerely. "Possessions are a tremendous responsibility," he added as a warning but he could tell by the blank expression of the student's face that he did not understand what he meant. After all, thought Michael, perhaps they would be very happy in a place like this. They would have exactly what they wanted. How naïve I've been about my feelings. I've expected others to share the same reaction and have gotten angry when they have not. He was thinking specifically of Mona and how he had been avoiding her and almost ignoring the children simply because they did not understand how he felt. How could they when they did not feel the same way at all. How foolish he had been. How unfair. The ice clicked emptily in the student's glass. He smiled appreciatively in the darkness. Yes, the boy was under quite a strain. New bride. New surroundings. New situation on the couch. "You've got a very fine girl in Alice," he said because he wanted to bolster up the boy's sagging morale.

"Yes, sir," he said quickly, almost painfully. "I think so, sir. She says the same thing about you. I mean, what a fine person you are, sir."

The "sir" annoyed Michael considerably. He felt like a doddering old man. But he did not protest. The boy had enough troubles for one evening. "Shall we go in?" he asked finally.

"Yes, sir," came the prompt reply.

Michael winced but led the way in. At the very moment they started inside, both of them could clearly hear the Senator's raucous voice saying, "But you've got a beautiful figure, my dear. You could have the whole world at your feet." Including, Michael thought, the Senator. He was disconcerted to notice that the Senator had placed an investigating hand on Alice Grant's charming shoulder. He turned quickly to see if the boy had noticed. From the rigid set of his jaw, Michael realized he had. In order to distract his attention, he took the boy's empty glass. "I'll get you another," he grinned.

"You know, Michael," called out Mrs. Drake across the room. There was a tinge of desperation in her voice. "The Senator and I are planning to go to Europe in July. Why don't you and Mona come along? We'd love to have you." Then she added loudly, "Wouldn't we, Senator?"

"What's that, my dear?" said the Senator, breaking away from his conversation momentarily, and at the same time pulling his investigating hand down to his side. "Yes, why, of course we would. Couldn't think of anything we'd like better."

And I, thought Michael exasperatedly, couldn't think of anything worse. The Senator would be running around the decks like an old-time Hollywood comic chasing after the pretty girls. "Not this year," he said politely. "Maybe another time." He noticed the disappointed expression on Mona's face. For some reason he was disturbed by it. "I just can't get away now," he explained apologetically. He glanced straight at her. "I've got a very important case coming up in the next two or three months." He knew she was not convinced. He stopped. He turned away from his wife's incriminating gaze. He reached out for his empty glass and filled it half full of whiskey.

"Maybe," joked the Senator mischievously, turning around to Alice who still sat comfortably nestled in the corner of the couch. "Maybe you'd like to go with us, my dear?" He laughed uproariously and at the same time he slapped her knee lightly but with an intimate suggestion.

Suddenly, in the far corner where no one had been looking, the student slammed down his glass angrily and said loudly, "Alice, I'm going now."

There was an immediate silence. Each one of them seemed frozen in the position they were in before he had spoken. Alice blushed painfully. Mrs. Drake clutched at her necklace. The Senator stopped laughing. Mona looked to Michael for help.

But to Michael's relief and surprise, Alice Grant saved the situation. She stood up, blonde and lovely and competent. "Why, Senator," she said in a joking tone, "I'd just love to go with you but what would we *do* with my husband?" Again there was awkward pause. The Senator's eyes blinked rapidly. He couldn't quite tell if she was or wasn't making fun of him. She turned towards her husband and gave him a long, loving smile that brought an overjoyed expression to his face, an expression Michael had seen many times on Annette's face whenever he was going to offer her a bone. "We've had a lovely time," she said to Mona, smiled hesitantly at Mrs. Drake, then turned to Michael. "Thank you, Mr. Humphrey," she said pleasantly. With a humorous glint in her eye she added, "It's been quite an experience." Michael realized instinctively that she had, in her way, been enjoying the Senator's appreciation, that she had not been disturbed by it in the least. At the door she turned back and called to the Senator, "When they have the next election, Senator, you can count on me to campaign for you."

"Well, really," exclaimed Mrs. Drake as the door closed.

Michael had to laugh. The Senator was very proud of himself.

"Maybe the Senator would like another drink, Michael," suggested Mona. "I've got to go check on the children."

"Sure would," he said, hopping energetically about the room. He stayed out of his wife's grasping range. "But first I want to go to the little boys' room."

"You know where it is, Senator," Michael said, refilling his glass.

"Sure ought to know it by now." With a humorous smile on his face he danced up the stairs.

Mrs. Drake sat back in the chair looking irritated and just a little bit tired. The way her lips puckered, Michael thought perhaps she was on the verge of tears. Unexpectedly she glanced over at him for reassurance.

"I'm sorry," she said quietly. "He just never seems to grow up, does he? He acts like a silly old man the moment he sees a pretty girl. I don't care, you understand. It's just that sometimes it's so humiliating to see him behave so idiotically." She took out a small handkerchief from her bag.

"I think Alice understood," he said, remembering that humorous glint.

"Oh, yes, I'm sure she did. She understood that he was just a silly old fool but because he's a Senator she has to sit there all evening and listen to all that adolescent nonsense of his."

Michael bit his lips nervously. He was hoping that Mona would come back soon. He always hated situations where, for the moment, social and human barriers were removed and replaced with unexpected honesty and candor. So the Senator *was* an old fool. But did it have to be said aloud? Think it, but certainly there was no need to mention it. Sometimes, there was something so disfiguring about honesty.

He hear Mrs. Drake saying, "I wonder what *they* would think of him if they could see him like this?"

He turned towards her. "Who?"

"The people who voted for him," she said seriously. "What would they think?"

Michael knew damn well what they would think. More than any other people in the world, Americans were more concerned with the private life of their celebrities and statesmen. They don't care about ability or intelligence, in fact, either one of those could lose an election for the candidate, but they did care about their moral behavior. As long as their personal life was family life and there were no scandalous skeletons in the closet, a nominee was in the clear, he had a chance. When he glanced up, he was relieved to see Mona standing in the doorway watching. "Would you like another drink?" he asked. She shook her head.

Mrs. Drake stood up impatiently. "I'm going home, Mona. You can tell him when he comes down that I'm waiting for him to take me out to dinner." She put her fur piece around her neck hastily. "As usual, my dear, it was good being here with both of you." She patted Mona's cheek affectionately. "You're so fortunate having such a wonderful husband like Michael instead of what I've got upstairs. You'll never know how fortunate."

Mona glanced meaningfully over at Michael. "I think I know," she said proudly. "Let me see you to the door, Bea."

Left alone, Michael decided to have another drink. When he heard the Senator close the door upstairs he was determined not to be in the living room when he came down, so he took his highball and sneaked out into the garden. The darkness hung about him like a conspirator's cloak. Stars flickered brightly like newly polished diamonds. The big dipper looked upside down. And the milky way ran like a pasture full of white flowers across the lower half of the sky. As he sat down, he could feel the cool breezes washing faintly up against his cheeks. The surface of the table was slightly moist. The grass beneath his feet felt soft and cushiony. *Why*, he asked himself for the hundreth time, should I want to get away from all of this? What *am* I after? What's the matter with me? Where will my discontent lead me? He closed his eyes wearily, then rubbed them gently with his finger tips.

And that young woman? What was she after? Something? He could not tell. Did she know? And why had he behaved so oddly about not wanting to believe what she had said about having just come from a convent? What did that mean? He recalled her exact tone of voice when she had said, "Is there something I can do to help you?" Help me? And when he had asked her why she thought he needed help how simply she had replied, "Something does." As if she damned well knew what it was. That's what irritated him. She probably *did* know what was the matter with him. He remembered how her eyes had looked straight into his, knowing, yet not knowing his secret. There was a quietness about her that soothed him, that made him feel irrationally safe. Where was she now? he wondered. What was she doing?

He had never known a religious of any sort. He had seen nuns, two by two mostly, walking together in Paris or Germany, and true, he had wondered what kind of a life they led. But they were always worlds apart. He never had thought of them as human beings. They were removed. Dedicated. And their veils and clicking beads, their modest glances and pale lips were all a part of another world behind thick doors and high walls.

Only once, on a train in England, could he recall having talked directly to a nun. He was sitting in a compartment reading, when two nuns entered, asked if they might share the space, pulled in a large black bag with shiny handles, sat down, chatted nervously in slight whispers as if they were in a hospital, then finally the older, plumper one took out her frayed prayer book and began to read. The other, as far as he could tell, was younger, her cheeks were rosy, her eyes full of curiosity, for he found her several times watching him carefully. He smiled. She smiled back. The older nun glanced up. They both turned away. Then the older nun went back to reading her book with the intensity of a farmer plowing under the earth. He went back to his book. She went back to looking straight ahead. Then about fifteen minutes later he was aware of a soft snoring sound. Looking up he found that the older nun had plowed herself under in sleep. The younger nun blushed. Apologetically she glanced over at him for the other nun's snoring. He smiled quickly to assure her that he did not mind in the least. She smiled her thanks. Those eyes of hers were fill of repressed mirth. He felt at any moment she would burst into laughter.

He couldn't help himself. He had to ask, "Are you *forbidden* to smile?"

"To smile?" she repeated softly, so as not to wake her companion. "No," she said lightly, happily. "No, we are *encouraged* to smile." And with that she gave him the happiest, most charming smile he had seen in a long time. "There," she said, full of amusement.

But before he could reply, the older nun woke up abruptly,

looked suspiciously from her companion to him, and said briskly, "Sister, I hope you've been saying your rosary."

"Indeed I have been, Sister," she replied earnestly.

The old nun clutched up her book again. The train went on chucking along. The younger nun made slight motions with her lips as if she was indeed saying her rosary. However, just before they left, after the older nun had thanked him, the younger nun turned and said, "And sir, I do hope you've been saying your rosary too." She gave him that charming smile, then they were gone. He sat there laughing. He had no idea that nuns could be so human, so full of humor.

"You mean to tell me that Bea went home without me?" he could hear the Senator asking in a hurt tone.

Michael took a long swallow from his highball, hoping that the liquor would soften his thoughts that lingered like late-afternoon shadows. So she had come from a convent. How pathetic she looked with the black dress, those washed-out eyes, that wan smile, yet there was much more to her than that. There was something so melodramatic about her situation. She seemed so terribly willing to help, even perfect strangers. She was too open, too vulnerable to life. He had not asked her how she came to realize that she had no vocation. He had not asked her a great many questions that he had thought of later. Somehow he would have to find her again. Maybe she went for walks there every afternoon. In some way he was certain of, she held an explanation for him. He had to find that explanation at all costs.

He had no idea of how long he had been sitting there when he became aware of his wife standing with her arms folded in the doorway. "Hi," he said self-consciously, rattling the ice in the glass. "Been getting a little air."

"The Senator left," she said lightly. "I don't think I ever remember Bea walking out on him like that before."

"She should have done it a long time ago," he said,

chuckling to himself.

"He doesn't mean any harm," she said, walking towards her husband. "He's actually quite harmless. He just plays at the part of being Casanova." She touched his arm lightly, experimenting to see how he might react to her nearness. "He just wants to be liked, that's all."

"He's pretty old for that kind of behavior, isn't he?" He was aggravated because his wife seemed so willing to overlook the Senator's childish behavior. He moved his arm partially away from her touch.

She stood there trying to make up her mind what step she should take next. "Michael, what's the matter now? Have I done something wrong?" She was getting to the point where she could no longer stand his indifference. Sometimes she felt that he had actually blotted her out of his mind.

"Of course not," he said matter-of-factly.

"What is it then?" She sat down in the chair next to his, making certain that she did not touch him. "Is it me?"

He turned his head. In the half darkness he could see the outline of her face, felt her eyes studying his every move, questioning his tone, fretting about his words until he became angry. I'm getting to feel that I'm under some kind of surveillance. Perhaps now would be the best time to offer her some explanation. "Mona," he began, hoping to be honest. "I don't really know what is the matter with me. I suddenly feel cheated in some way even I don't understand. I'm just not positive enough about what I do feel. Sometimes I get the impression that my life is slipping away and what have I done with it? What have I got to show for it? Where did I go to?"

"But you're a successful lawyer, Michael," she said boastfully. "You've got a lovely home and lovely children. Why, you've got about as much as any man your age has, if not a great deal more."

"I don't mean that kind of success," he tried to explain. "I mean a personal success. I'm not a success with myself. I've let myself slip away somewhere. Only I'm just becoming aware of it."

Michael knew his wife did not function too well in the world of the abstract. She had to handle, to feel the world she possessed between her capable fingers. Ideas never appealed to her. They were evasions. They stalled action. Action was her favorite occupation. Whenever Michael's or for that matter anyone else's conversation took on a philosophical tone, she shied away from continuing it. Instantly she was out of her depth. She only coped with what she could see – not with what she could imagine. She reached out longingly and touched the back of her husband's hand. "Darling let's go inside where we can talk about it properly. It's chilly out here."

He knew it was no use. "There's nothing really to talk about," he said sadly. "That's another thing. You have a passion for talking everything out. We don't seem to ever have time to feel anything anymore. We just discuss what we feel and what we don't feel until there's nothing left. We take the flavor away. It's as if we distrust each other's thoughts. We *must* know what the other is thinking. No one seems to have secrets anymore. We're all laid out like corpses on a table for each other to see and examine. No, I don't want to talk. That's the last thing I want to do now. Now I want to feel something."

"Sometimes," said his wife quietly, bitterly, with a touch of impatience in her voice, "I suspect I don't even know who you are."

He looked defensively over at her. "Sometimes, I don't even know who I am myself," he said softly.

She made no effort to reply. He sat there motionless. She glanced up at the stars, then back him. He picked up his glass and took another swallow. She watched him place the glass back down on the metal table. Finally, "I'm going to clean up the living room before I begin dinner." She stood up, hesitated, looked up once more at the stars, then went back inside. Without even turning he knew what she was doing. And he was right. She was busy emptying the ashtrays and collecting glasses. On her face he knew there would be a serious preoccupied frown. Again he was right. But he was very wrong in imagining what she was thinking. She had decided that things had gone as far as they could go. Now they had reached an impasse. Only time would tell the outcome.

Chapter Five

A softness had settled around them in the garden. Anna held her breath as a swift-flying swallow dipped and dove over the small pond at the end of the yard near the rose bushes. For a second, she recalled the first time that she and David had come to visit as children, and how they had gone down to the Five and Ten Cents store buying three or four small goldfish to stock it with. Each morning before breakfast, they would eagerly run down to the pond to make sure the fish were still there. What an uncomplicated world that had been! Everything seemed do be exactly what it was. A tree was a tree. A flower was a flower. Goldfish were just goldfish. But somehow, now, nothing seemed to be what it was anymore. Even she wasn't what she had supposed when she was younger. "Grandmother," Anna spoke up, breaking the stillness, shattering the momentary peace into little fragments. "Why is it that the world is so simple, so uncomplicated when you're young, but as you grow older it becomes more complex and disturbing?"

"Ah, my dear," exclaimed the older woman knowingly; she patted the arm of the wicker chair she was sitting in. "That's a question I've often pondered over myself."

"Did you ever find an answer?" asked Anna, turning her head towards her grandmother, who sat perfectly straight in her chair like an actress on the stage.

"Perhaps a near one," she replied, glancing intently down at the ground as if the answer were hidden somewhere in the grass. "I think it's got a great deal to do with what we want out of life. Or rather, what we think we need to make us happy. When we're children we accept life for what it is. We enjoy the excitement it has to offer. But as we grow older we begin to make demands on life. We must have money. We must have love. We must have security. We begin to set goals for ourselves. Then we begin to demand from each other."

"I suppose the best way to put it would be," suggested Anna, "that when we're children we live in a foolish sort of Paradise."

Mrs. Ross nodded her head in agreement. "I can remember perfectly how Mama used to tell us in order to grow up we would have to leave our Paradise. "Some of us," she used to say, "would never let go of it. Some of us couldn't wait to get away. Others would hesitate forever. But whatever we did, wherever we went, we would be continually trying to re-create that original Paradise all over again, but it would never quite be the same as our first one." Her voice faltered. In a whisper she continued, "Then sometimes death comes along to destroy even that second Paradise." She was thinking of her husband, who had been dead for over five years. "What does one do without it? Where does one go? Whom does one turn to?"

Anna had turned to Christ but suddenly she realized that that Paradise was no longer hers. Yes, where was she to find another?

"Yes," went on her grandmother, eloquent with recollection. "Each one of us holds on to or lets go of the Paradise of our childhood just like Adam and Eve had to. We have to abandon it sooner or later."

"But," protested Anna, "we *all* have a share in the Original Sin. We're all cast out of Paradise."

"My dear, that's only partially true," explained Mrs. Ross abruptly with a tinge of impatience in her voice. She was an Episcopalian and she disliked discussing religious problems with her Catholic granddaughter. "We may *all* be expelled from Paradise," she conceded knowingly, "but some of us hold on to it inside, as a place to go back to when we're tired and discouraged."

"Oh!" remarked Anna, preferring suddenly to change the subject. Her grandmother did have such odd ideas about religion. "Maybe we'd better talk about something else."

Mrs. Ross had become quite agitated but when she saw the strained expression on Anna's face she smiled cheerfully. "We should know better, you and I, than to discuss such matters." She changed her position slightly in the chair so that she could face her granddaughter squarely. "Tell me, my dear, what do you intend to do now?"

Anna shook her head in perplexion. "I don't know yet. I've tried not to even think about it. I guess...." she hesitated, "I guess I've lost another Paradise and I don't know where to find the next one."

"Why don't you go back to college?" suggested Mrs. Ross. I must remember to get her some new dresses Monday, she thought. I can't look at that dreary black dress day in and day out.

"Maybe I will," mumbles Anna. She lifted her head upward in order to watch the stars coming out one by one in the sky as if someone were on the other side sticking pins through it, first here, then there.

"Maybe you'll fall in love," said her grandmother casually.

"Maybe I will."

The idea seemed perfectly right for Anna somehow, thought Mrs. Ross. She was a terribly romantic girl. As far back as she could remember Anna, she had been mooning away, shy, yet full of deep feelings. After all, falling in love is just a state of mind. Mrs. Ross had decided that long, long ago. One simply wanted to fall in love. One worked oneself up into a frenzied state of mind. Then one found someone else who was in the same state, and there it was. Sometimes one had to coax another into that state of mind but in Anna's case, Mrs. Ross decided she was already in it, in fact, had been in it for years and years. She wouldn't be a bit surprised if she hadn't fallen in love with the idea of Christ. Only He just hadn't reciprocated. And Anna had felt spurned. "I think it would do you worlds of good if you did," commented her grandmother.

"Maybe it would." Her grandmother had hardly mentioned the word 'love' when she remembered the face of the man she had met in the park that afternoon. She had completely forgotten him up until now. Suddenly there he was again. She closed her eyes, saw the dog romping about the grass, then he was standing in front of her with his dark eyes and that pained expression on his face. She opened her eyes quickly. "Grandmother," she said, "I met the strangest man in Dumbarton Oaks this morning."

"What kind of a strange man?" she asked. Her flagging interest suddenly became renewed with curiosity.

"A very nice strange man actually," she said, smiling slightly. "He had a French poodle."

"What's the man's name?" she asked, wondering if he was someone she might know.

"I forgot to ask it."

"Was he attractive?"

"Yes," she hesitated. "Yes, he was very attractive. One of the handsomest men I've ever seen. But there was something sad about him, something that made me want to help him. He interested me very much."

There was something in Anna's voice that interested Mrs. Ross too. "What did you two talk about?" she asked, careful not to sound too interested.

"We talked about different things." She had difficulty in remembering. "One thing I do remember was that he simply refused at first to believe me when I told him I had just gotten out of a convent. Maybe he was just joking. But he said that when he didn't want to believe something he could force himself not to."

"We all do that," admitted Mrs. Ross. "But why should he disbelieve what you told him? He's never seen you before, has he? That's very odd of him." Apprehensively she reached out touch her granddaughter's arm. "Anna, you must be very careful who you talk to in Dumbarton. Dreadful things happen there all the time. Young girls get swallowed up in parks. Weeks later the police find them covered up with leaves. Then sometimes, my dear, dreadful sex things happen. Kind old men turn out to be worse than fiends."

Anna laughed. "Really, Grandmother, you're so wonderful. If you would just hear how you sound. So ominous."

"You have only to read the newspapers in the morning to see how right I am." She folded her arms grandly, stood up unexpectedly, looked skyward, then said reverently, "How much God must love us. He's given us such a beautiful world to live in."

The soft sound of her grandmother's voice filled Anna with a sudden, swift desire for closeness, and with a quickness that startled the older woman, Anna threw her arms about her, hugging her hungrily. "I'm so glad I'm here with you," she said, choking back tears.

"There, there, my dear," said her grandmother, patting her back soothingly. "Everything's going to be all right, you'll see. Life will work it out somehow. It just takes time in the beginning. We all must start somewhere. We must trust ourselves a little more." They stood motionless like this, neither one speaking, each thinking very personal thoughts, each pleased with the proximity of the other until finally Mrs. Ross disengaged herself. "I've got one or two calls to make before I retire. I asked Mary to make us some of her delicious hot cocoa. We'll have some before we go to bed. It will make you sleep better."

After her grandmother had disappeared inside, Anna sat

down again. Darkness hugged the corners of the yard and covered the bushes and trees like dust covers draped over furniture. Every now and again she could hear the last chirps coming from the swallows as they settled down in their clay nests. Yes, she thought, God had given them such a beautiful world to live in. This was her first night out of the convent. The walls were gone. The safeness passed, yet she had to admit that in many ways she felt far closer to God sitting quietly in the yard than she ever had praying to His Son. Now, even though there were only warm breezes touching the trees and quick movements of birds stirring in the bushes, there was life here, and in the end, wasn't she on the side of life? When she thought of the night before, how she had stayed in her room feeling remorseful and lost, she smiled because she had been so apprehensive. Think of all the nights when I cried my way through until morning. How she had begged and begged Christ for guidance. Then finally that guidance had come in the shape of Sister Mary Thomas, who had come in one night about three weeks ago and said gently, "Anna, why don't you give in?"

"Give in," she had cried angrily. "Give in to what?"

Sister Mary had said quietly, inoffensively, "Give in to the truth."

She had sat up defiantly on the edge of her bed, ready to fight back. "What truth? I don't know what you're talking about, Sister."

"I've been watching you now for these past several weeks. I've seen the torment you're putting yourself through. Anna, it's only your pride that's holding you back. You're simply afraid to admit that you've made a wrong choice."

"Sister, please let me alone. Please."

After the nun had left, she had stayed awake all night, never sleeping, only lying there numb and unhappy. Now, everyone knew.

The next morning after breakfast she had gone in to see

Mother Superior. She could still remember that patient look on her face as she waited for Anna to speak.

"Yes, Sister, what is it?"

She had taken a long breath because she realized that once she uttered the words, her whole life would be changed, her future completely different than the one she had planned for. "I want to leave the convent. I don't have the vocation I thought I had."

"You are certain of that?"

"Yes, Mother," she said, nodding her head. "I am now."

So, here she was, sitting out in the garden in Georgetown. Her words had led her straight to this spot. Two Paradises gone. Where was the next one to come from? After all, until Eve came on the scene, Adam was living in a garden. Once she was there, the garden became a Paradise. So perhaps she would have to find her Adam.

"Maybe you'll fall in love," echoed her grandmother's words.

Now she shook her head. "No, I'm too weak for love. I couldn't bear it." But at the same time she recalled his face, and the expression that begged her for sympathy. His eyes seemed to be burning through the darkness into hers. Disconcerted by her imagination, she stood up quickly and, taking one last look at the garden, ran inside.

Chapter Six

On the following Thursday around ten after ten, a car from the Pentagon stopped by to pick up Michael Humphrey. As it sped along Fourteenth Street past the Jefferson Memorial, the driver spoke. "The cherry trees are beginning to bloom, sir," he said proudly.

Michael looked up from the *Post* he was reading while the driver obligingly slowed down so he could see the view. Yes, he saw that they were beginning to blossom but he thought the entire affair was a dismal fiasco. The endless photographs in the newspapers, the continual treadmill for tourists who herded themselves in by the thousands, laughing, eating, sweating, taking pictures of each other posing against the background of the basin or holding down a branch of the pale pink blossoms as if they were posing for a screen test. As far as he could tell, no one ever noticed the trees, nor the fragile charm of sunlight shining on the paper-thin petals. Instead, they gorged themselves with hot dogs and orange pop, or cuddled romantically, kissing and pawing each other as if they were out in the bushes. There were ice cream vendors and soft drink vendors crying their wares. There were soldiers and sailors hunting for a pick up. No, he wanted no part of it. As he looked out the window, it seemed incredible that such a gentle beauty from the necklace of trees that surrounded the small, placid basin of water, would, in a few days, be turned into a sideshow, a tourist bedlam. He recalled with distaste how, that first year after they had moved to Georgetown, Mona kept nagging at him to take her and the children down to see the trees when they came out. And he had, of course, in the end, given in. But he had never forgotten it.

As the government car sped towards the Fourteenth Street bridge, he put his paper aside, because he remembered another incident very much like the one that had occurred with Mona. He must have been around ten or eleven when it happened. It was in 1960, the year his grandparents had taken his whole family to Europe, financing the entire trip because they said they had a fear that their children might go through life insulated and mentally cramped.

One morning, in Paris, his grandmother suddenly decided that she wanted to see the Shrine at Lourdes. However, no one, including his grandfather, who said that medieval mysticisms bored him, consented to go along. Ruthlessly, she recruited Michael. "It's a place were a *true* miracle happened," she had told him, her eyes wide open with astonishment.

"What's a true miracle?" he had asked reluctantly, watching her stick a long, sharp pin in the crown of a large velvet hat. He imagined by the way she pushed the pin in quickly that the point of it ran right through her skull.

"A true miracle is when," she took a deep breath, still glancing with admiration at herself in the mirror, "something that *can't* happen *does*." She smiled at her simple explanation, then turning around she must have found a frown on his face. "Well, what is it, Michael?" She pulled nervously at her white gloves, pulling them down tightly over her small hands.

"I don't understand," he said in puzzlement.

"But my dear, that's the whole *point* to a miracle." She patted his shoulder affectionately. "No one *understands* it! Now say you'll come along with grandmother. We'll have a lovely ride on one of those funny little French trains. We'll see fields of cabbages and little toy houses along the way."

He accepted with pleasure because there was something

about being with his grandmother that he enjoyed. She had a wonderful way of making exciting things happen.

Lourdes was a strange, many-angled town, with steep streets jutting out then disappearing abruptly. He could still remember the feel of the cobbled stones beneath his feet, and once he stopped to look in the windows of a butcher's shop where hares hung upside down, with dark rivulets of blood dripping out of their black noses. In another he saw a decapitated pig's head that was a bright pink, its eyes closed peacefully as if the pig were dreaming a very pleasant dream.

On the morning they got up to go to the Shrine, his grandmother began telling him the story of Bernadette as their rickety taxi chugged along the twisting streets. "This young girl was tending some sheep or something when she had a vision."

"What's a vision?"

She became irritated. "Must you be eternally asking what this is or what that is?" She stopped suddenly, looking down at his forlorn face. "I'm sorry, my dear, I keep forgetting how young you are. And how much older I am. Questions are for the young, I suppose." She took a deep breath. "Well, let's see. A vision is when something that's *there* isn't."

"Like what?" he asked, more baffled than before.

"Well, my dear," she said, becoming more disconcerted by the minute. "Must you always be so specific? Well, let's see. I have it. Like the moon. You can't see it now but it's up there in the sky just the same. If you said you could *see* it now and it really wasn't *there* ... well, Michael, that's a *vision*."

"I see...." he said doubtfully. He was completely aware of the fact that his grandmother was becoming more agitated as they got nearer their destination. He was not certain if his questions caused the agitation or the Shrine.

"Anyway," she went on to say, "this young girl saw this vision of the Virgin and–"

"What's a virgin?" he asked.

"Really, Michael," she said in a low, controlled voice, making sure that the driver could not overhear. "Are you deliberately trying to be funny? She saw this vision of Jesus' mother."

"Oh?" he whispered.

"Anyway, where she saw this vision, a spring has, well, I guess you'd say, sprung up miraculously. People come from all parts of the world to expose themselves to it. They buy it in bottles and sometimes the water heals them. The travel book says there are miracles here every day."

"How," he asked shyly, "do you make a miracle happen?"

"I think, my dear," she said reverently, "That you must *believe* it happened. And in the world we live in now, belief is fast disappearing. As the years pass, I think it will become more and more difficult to believe in anything or anybody."

The cab came to a sudden halt. After paying the fare, his grandmother got out, he following, and they found themselves in what Michael first thought was a large market place, for there were different-sized booths in all directions, only, instead of selling farm produce, they were offering as their wares, silver and gold medals, rosaries strung up by the hundreds like the hares he had seen in the butcher shop, some black, some made of flat brown cocoa beans, others richly glittering in gold and silver. There were booths selling statues of a woman in blue with her arms spread open wide as if she wanted to cover the whole world with sympathy. Other booths sold candles alone. Some were squatty, others beautifully ornamented. Some were plain for the poor. But it was the sweet, clean smell of the beeswax that Michael enjoyed most of all. The scent permeated the whole booth and filled the air with this delicate odor. Next, he noticed a booth that sold strange, grotesque-shaped medals which turned out to be, on closer inspection, various parts of the human body, arms, legs, kidneys, hearts, spleens, hands, beribboned, and, as he later learned, they were to be pinned onto the bases of statues in the church. There was something frightening to Michael about this ritual. The idea of it disconcerted him but his grandmother took an amusing view of the matter.

"My dear, it's very much like pinning your hopes to something," she said. But even then he had found the matter distasteful.

They were suddenly caught up in a pushing, milling crowd of pilgrims who were heading up some well-worn steps. (Was it the image of the crowds from the Jefferson Memorial that brought this recollection back into his consciousness?) Many of the women wore black scarves pulled tightly around their chins. They were praying audibly, some kissing their clicking, finger-worn rosaries ardently. Michael held tightly to his grandmother's hand but there were times when the crowd surged forth and parted them.

As they neared the Shrine, Michael smelled the scent of incense in the air, and up ahead hundreds of candles gleamed in a grotto. He turned to show his grandmother but he was startled to find that her face had become tense, her lips tightly clamped, her eyes staring straight ahead. Her breathing had become deeper. In some unexplained way, she had suddenly removed herself from him. She was next to him, yet she was not. She was no longer the person he had been with, and he became frightened. Quickly he let go of her warm, gloved hand. (He wondered now as he sat in the car, *what* miracle she had been hoping to believe in?)

Nervously he glanced around at the hundreds of other people, noticed two or three men on crutches straining and perspiring, trying to keep up with the crowd. He saw one small girl with a candle burning feebly in her hand. The crowd swayed as if it were a wheat field smitten by a strong wind, Suddenly they fell to their knees, and as they did so, he saw clearly up ahead, suspended, it seemed to him, in midair, amid smoky candlelight, the Virgin. Once again he turned to his grandmother to show her, but he found that she, too, was on her knees, and in her white gloved hands she held a black rosary which she had evidently bought at one of the stands when he was not looking.

"Grandmother?" he called softly, trying to attract her attention.

Instead of replying, she simply put her hand on his shoulders and forced him down on his knees with the rest.

Out of nowhere came a blaze of singing. Snatches of it sprung up here and there in the crowd, their ardor fanning the singing into a burning crescendo of adoration and prayer. The upturned faces, dimly lit by candles, pleaded hopefully for blessings.

As Michael listened, he was aware for the very first time in his life that he was deeply afraid, afraid from a fear he had never before experienced. Here, he was surrounded by adults on all sides, including his grandmother, especially his grandmother, all adults who made up what the world was to him, adults whom he believed in and trusted, whom he assumed knew what they were doing with their adult world, only before his very eyes, they had become stripped of their solidarity, their self-assurance, their certainty, and had gone down on their knees pleading for help before the Shrine.

Perhaps it was this naked, unrestrained admittance that they needed help that stunned him deeply, for if *they* were not certain, if they were not sure of what they were doing, who was? In that very instant, his whole outlook on life changed completely, finally.

He had placed his belief and trust in adults, who now on all sides of him betrayed that belief and that trust. In that instant, his whole viewpoint of the world he lived in collapsed, never to be recovered. An inner rebellion made him angry because he had been betrayed by adults. They were not at all what they seemed to be. Their individualism had been swallowed up in a wave of mass emotion, letting him out of it, alone and afraid.

How long they had stayed down on their knees singing he never did know. Now he no longer wanted his grandmother's hand for support. He would have to support himself in the future as best he could. Events began to come back into focus once he and his grandmother were in a cab going back to his hotel. Neither one spoke until, inadvertently, his grandmother changed her position on the seat. As she did so, the rosary she had been using fell to the floor. Pointedly, he bent over to pick the beads up.

"I didn't see you buy these," he said accusingly, handing them over to her.

She sensed his resentment. "You were too busy looking at the candles."

"Did you *see* any miracle?" he asked tauntingly.

She shook her head, reached over and put her arm affectionately about his shoulders. "No ... but I prayed."

"What for?"

"Strength to go on believing," she admitted honestly. "I'm not a Catholic, it's true, but I prayed anyway. There was a heavy feeling in the air with all those candles glittering hopefully up in the Shrine. And all of those poor people praying. I don't know. I just prayed. The feeling was too heavy to evade. After all, who knows, maybe she *did* see the Virgin. Maybe she had belief enough in her vision. Maybe there really *was* a miracle." Suddenly she stopped talking, smiled at Michael and was about to suggest that they catch the first train back to Paris when she thought of something. "My goodness, Michael, we forgot to get some of the water to take back to your mother. We came all this way and forgot it. Shall I ask the driver to turn around and go back?"

"No!" he shouted fiercely. "No.... I don't ever want to go back there. I hate that place. I hate Shrines."

And I still do, he thought to himself in the back of the car. I hate Shrines of any sort. The sun shone on the snow white surface of the Jefferson Memorial, making it glisten like a mirage shimmering in the distance. Just as the car turned the last curve before the bridge, he saw a bus had pulled over to the side and high school children were piling out. Hanging on the side of the bus was a makeshift banner saying 'Cherry blossoms or bust'. He shook his head sadly. Perhaps, after all, it was not the shrines that he disliked as much as what people *did* to them.

The face of his grandmother came back for a moment, that tense expectancy etched strongly into it, the lips pulled tightly together, the breathing deepened. Yes, there was no doubt that she, too, had been hoping for a miracle. His grandmother was dead now. Both his parents gone. He very seldom, if ever, looked back to yesterday.

In that respect he was very much American. He concentrated on the here and the now. He could not afford the luxury of examining the past; only, in all honesty, he was bored with what he had been concentrating on so conscientiously. He was perfectly aware of the prevalent theory that today made the tomorrow. Yet, when he glanced around at what man had done today, ignoring the material and scientific advancement, considering more what he had been doing to himself and the human spirit, his only thought was, what would tomorrow be like?

From the looks of today, tomorrow would never even exist, or if it did, man would not be there to appreciate it. But I suppose, he thought philosophically, man has been thinking this since the beginning of his conscious history. (Wasn't history one of man's attempts at permanency?) The Neanderthal must have reacted the same way when he saw the huge masses of ice creeping down from the north, crushing under it all life, and whatever civilization there was.

But in the end, sitting there in the car, he realized in all honesty that deep inside he, too, had been hoping for a miracle of some sort, for a personal reassurance that God *was* in His Heaven, that he, Michael, was of some importance, a purpose to living. I suppose all man has ever wanted was just a little reassurance that there *was* a purpose to living. And I guess that's what a miracle is for. To reassure man that there *is*. To make him feel that God is still there. Still caring, still vitally interested in his progress. Even if He wasn't there, man would have to go on bringing miracles into existence in order to stabilize himself in the universe that shows a steady disconcerting indifference to his future. Now, for the first time in history, man actually has possession of that future. It lay within the confines of an atom, the smallest unit of energy in the universe. Michael laughed. Surely there was something tragically humorous about man's situation.

Only that miracle has never come. Perhaps, he thought suddenly, excited by the very idea of it, perhaps I must *make* my own miracle happen. Perhaps, like Bernadette, I must *believe* in my own vision. I must give a purpose to my own existence. When Michael thought back on his childhood he could swear that within his lifetime the location of God and His world had disintegrated. When he was younger, he knew that the sky held God and His saints and angels. Now, he knew there were only planets, and endless constellations and beautiful floating nebulae circling the earth. Where had God gone to? Where else was He safe? Then in a lightening flash he thought he understood where God was hiding now. His last resort. And Michael was suddenly comforted and terrified at the same time.

Chapter Seven

Anna finally gave in. All week long her grandmother has been urging her to buy some new dresses.

"Anna, dear, really you must have some lighter dresses. Black is such an unflattering color for a girl your age. You must let me make an appointment to have your hair done. I'm going to send you straight to Neiman's. You can charge whatever you like. But I want to see you in something charming and yellow."

In the beginning, she had refused flatly to even consider her grandmother's suggestion.

"But why?" her grandmother asked her over and over again. "What harm is there in looking attractive?"

The actual fact was, in a way, Anna did feel that too much attention to one's physical appearance was wrong, almost bordering on sinfulness. Modesty was certainly one of the most important virtues the nuns had endeavored to instill into the novice. Wasn't that the whole point to the thick, unfashionable, uncomfortable skirts and hidden waists? Wasn't that why the hair was shorn, hair that was one of woman's most important assets, and the face furtively hidden by a starched wimple? Wasn't that why mirrors were all but extinct so that they would not be tempted to primp and pry into their physical charms? Hadn't she tried desperately for many months to keep all thoughts of her body, any awareness of it, out of her consciousness? And hadn't she found that the body, like a young child, refused to be placed in the background? In the end, wasn't vanity the religious main problem, the subduing of the flesh, the stamping out of the self, the greedy self?

She could still recall with shame the one morning before Matins when she had awakened; instead of rising immediately and kneeling by her bedside, she had lingered (or had the devil prompted her to?) and in that one unguarded moment she had touched her firm breasts and wondered how she would feel nursing a baby. Here was her grandmother asking her to give in to the temptations she had been fighting so hard to control.

True, several times in the past few days, she had found herself tempted to glance into the various mirrors scattered throughout the house. She had decided that perhaps she was not as plain as she had remembered. She wondered what she might look like with redder lips and a more fashionable hair style. But she still refused her grandmother's suggestions. The issue was clouded until one afternoon in the kitchen, Mary put her finger on the sore spot.

Anna had been out in the kitchen helping her shell peas for dinner. In the past few days an informal sort of relationship had sprung up between them, but each one was still uncertain of how the other would react.

"I done heard your grandmother after you again while you was eating your breakfast," Mary said casually, neither sympathizing nor condemning.

"Poor Grandmother," said Anna.

"Honey," Mary said, stopping her shelling, "I know it ain't none of my business, but your grandmother don't have too many pleasures left in her life. I knows you'd like to give her some. She'd be mighty pleased if you did what she asked you to."

"But," Anna retorted irritably, "I don't think that's a very valid reason to do something. It might give her pleasure but it would make me very uncomfortable."

"And just why's that, child?" Mary's shrewd eyes watched her face with interest.

"Just because it does, that's all," she said evasively.

Mary put down the pan she was holding in her lap. She hesitated, then decided that she had been given the opportunity to instruct so she took it. "Let me tell you a story about myself, honey, then maybe you can see what I mean. When I was just a young child, maybe eleven or so, my mama worked for some white folks out in Maryland. They lived on this here farm in the summer and Mama used to go out there each year. Sometimes I went to help on weekends. We'd make ice cream in a freezer. Had fried chicken seems to me every other day. Well, the Carsons, that was their names too, had a daughter just about my age with pretty blond hair and always dressed nice. One summer her mama decided to give her a birthday party. For some reason she asks Mama to ask me to come out for it. I liked Alice well enough when we was alone playing but when other white children came along she always acted uppity. When Mama told me that she wanted me to come out, I could tell by the way Mama smiled that she was happy I was invited. She even went down to buy me a dress to wear. It was made of a thin, crispy kind of pink material. As hard as I tried to make myself think different, I knew I just plain didn't want to go. I told Mama. Every day I told her I didn't want to go. She just couldn't understand why not. I told her, for one thing, I didn't want her to spend all that money on a dress I could only wear once or twice. Then I told her I didn't like Alice too well anyway. I told her every reason that came into my head why I didn't want to go. Except the right one.

"Finally, out in the kitchen one morning, she told me to sit down and listen. 'Do's ain't the reasons you don't want to go, is they?' she asks me. 'You knows they ain't.'

"I said, 'Well then you tell me the reason.' And honey, she did. Kept her voice down low and gave me the reason. 'You's ashamed of yourself, Mary Barton, that what you is. You's ashamed of yourself inside. You don't have no pride about you.

Not one bit. You's afraid to look nice and you makes me ashamed of you and me too.'

"Then Mama sat right down there in the kitchen and cried like I never seen her do before. I was going to tell her that she was wrong, but honey, I knew she done told the truth. I was *afraid* to go to that party. I was afraid they would make fun of me because I was colored.

Anna blushed noticeably. Mary's honesty disconcerted her. "But I don't see where there's any similarity," she said.

"I knew you wouldn't see, honey," laughed Mary pleasantly. "You is doing just what I did. Refusing to see. You is ashamed of yourself inside as I was. You is afraid to look pretty. That's it."

"Afraid to look pretty?" echoed Anna. The realization of the truth caused her to stand up.

"Honey, think of it this way. If God done put all them colors in the world like He put in the flowers and in the trees, why, I'm sure He wouldn't have no objection to you putting some on too."

Yes, admitted Anna, she supposed she *was* ashamed of herself. Not so much ashamed exactly. She really didn't have too much *belief* in her own beauty. Behind this lack of belief was a basic fear of competing with other women in the feminine world. She had never tried really to look attractive. She had always stayed in the background as far as her mother was concerned, pale and silent. Maybe Mary was right after all. Maybe you had to believe you were beautiful to look beautiful. Maybe that was the secret. "I guess you're right, Mary," she said, smiling gratefully.

"I know I is, honey," replied the colored woman. Her eyes were full of admiration. "You got a pretty face and you got a nice figure for a girl your age. You is a pretty girl, honey. Believe Mary, she knows.

That night while they were having dinner, with Mary

hovering attentively in the background, she told her grandmother, "I think you might be right about the dresses, Grandmother, I'll go to Neiman's in the morning."

So she had gone the next day, and spent what she was certain was the whole morning looking at hundreds of dresses. Next she went to the beauty salon. As the perfumed, expensive creams were being applied to her face, she could not help but smile as she remembered the ill-smelling soaps the nuns used made from lard and lye. Then her hair was washed and cut with a Mr. Jean styling it to her 'soft' personality, as he told her excitedly. To please her grandmother she had decided to wear a yellow dress home. As she walked out into the yard towards her grandmother, she did quite honestly believe she had a surface sort of beauty.

"My dear," exclaimed her grandmother, "If you only knew how lovely you look. How fresh and pretty."

Then she hurried upstairs. When Mary saw her she threw up her hands with admiration and covered her face with an apron she was wearing. "Well, I declare," she kept saying over and over. Then she would peek out from behind the apron to take a longer look. "Honey, you appears to be just as delicious-looking as them lemon ices I makes for your grandmother. You looks good enough to eat."

Yet, somehow it was different when Anna stood alone in her bedroom. Sadly she untied the box with her black dress in it. She held the dress up in front of her, then stepped before a full-length mirror. She was alarmed when she realized that already she *felt* changed, could in fact, feel herself changing right then and there into a new personality. The black dress she held in her hand reminded her of an empty chrysalis that butterflies leave behind on twigs once they have taken flight into the air. She dropped the dress on the side of the bed, then went over to her dressing table. She smiled skeptically at herself in the mirror. Was she really beautiful? Or just pleasant to look at?

There must be different kinds of beauty. Perhaps, to appreciate oneself is not truly a sin. Maybe beauty only becomes a sin when you place too much importance on it, on how you look instead of how you feel inside. For the first time in her life she thought she could understand how a woman's beauty could stir up pride and secret vanity. She could understand, too, how beauty could be used as a weapon, as a bargaining factor in regards to men and money and power.

Then, out of nowhere, the faint face of Sister Mary Francis, a nun who, in Anna's opinion, possessed one of the most beautiful faces she had ever seen, smiled back at her through the mirror. Her skin was white with a faint tinge of red on the cheeks. Her lips were dark and her eyebrows were black. Her deep brown eyes held such a look of simplicity, of such gentleness, without pretense, without any sort of emotions disturbing the calm-like, open gaze. Anna had spent a great deal of time when she first went into the convent watching this nun with awe, especially when she received communion in the morning. Sister Mary would walk slowly to the railing, her head bowed reverently, but when she actually received the wafer (Anna had curiously watched her several times at this point), an expression passed over the nun's face, her skin became suffused with an inner glow of some kind, perhaps ecstasy, her lips parted, then her eyes would look longingly up at the picture of Christ, eyes flooded with fulfillment. Anna would have to turn away because her envy was too great. Why could not this kind of beauty, this kind of longing possess her too?

Anna remembered the many times she and the other novices had discussed Sister Mary among themselves. They were all struck by the beauty, the inner beauty that was reflected on her face. She heard reports that the nun was particularly favored with God's grace. There were whispered rumors that she had the makings of a saint. But she was carefully watched by the rest of the community so that she did not go too far over in that direction. But no matter what was said about her, no one could take away the expression on her face, the beauty of it.

One thing Anna had noticed in particular the last few days was how few faces she saw looked happy. They were all intense faces, worried, unsure faces, with lines and drawn lips. Smiles were rare out in the world. Warmth completely gone. She glanced at herself in the mirror. Yes, her face was beginning to look the same. Attractive on the surface but nothing underneath. Nothing behind the eyes except worry. Self-absorption. That was it. No one seemed to care any longer about anyone else. Love could kindle that spark in the soul. Love could light up the inner being until its rays would be reflected in the eyes, on the lips, over the skin. Yes, she thought excitedly, love could do it. But who would need her love? Who would feel the same as she? Who else was searching for someone to love? Her thoughts went back to Dumbarton Oaks. Would there be a chance that he might return? Did he walk there every day? She had nothing to lose. And, perhaps, love to gain. Quickly she smiled at herself in the mirror. "Why not?" she said aloud. Her reflection offered no opposition.

Chapter Eight

Periodically, like homing pigeons winging their stolid way back to base, Mona Humphrey and Beatrice Drake flew together for a momentary pause in their social flight, about once every two weeks over a dietary luncheon neither cared about eating but did so anyway as an excuse for discussion. Mona unburdened herself by talking shatteringly of trivial or impersonal problems, sometimes skirting dangerously near topics of a more intimate nature, but whenever she did so, an inner reticence would pull her away from the subject. Beatrice, however, believed in directness and would unhesitatingly drop her burden exhaustedly at Mona Humphrey's feet, sighing, with stooped shoulders, a visual clue that the burden had gotten too heavy. While Mona continued to bear hers stoically, dropping every now and then a straw or two, Beatrice Drake always left the luncheon table relieved, cleansed, so to speak, as if she had been imbibing in the confessional.

This had been their position and routine since they had inaugurated their luncheon ritual over seven years ago, but as Beatrice Drake watched Mona coming towards her, she realized with relief and amusement that their tradition was about to collapse. Something unusual was wrong with her friend. She could see it in the hurried way she walked, in the tense manner in which she carried herself, as if, already, her burden had come undone and the straw was scattering loosely behind her.

"My dear," the senator's wife exclaimed affectionately, patting the arm of the empty chair for her friend to sit in. "What a divine hat you're wearing."

Mona smiled her polite thanks for the compliment. "Thanks, Bea," she remarked dourly, "but it's last year's."

What was that disturbed look about her eyes? wondered Mrs. Drake. Troubled look, the novels always said. "Do you feel all right, Mona?" She dug right into the middle of it, for she never had too much patience with preliminary measures.

"Feel all right?" echoed Mona Humphrey innocently. She stopped, however, in the middle of pulling off her gloves. "What makes you ask?"

"My dear," grinned Mrs. Drake, "I can read you like a book. A lovely open book. I see trouble, don't I? In big black letters. With lots of exciting footnotes."

"Maybe you do," conceded Mona.

"Then tell me what it is. Nothing to do with me, I hope?" She led her into troubled waters gradually like an expert Baptist minister leading his convert into baptism.

"No," smiled Mona wearily. "Nothing to do with you in the least." She glanced around the restaurant for a waitress. She needed a cocktail. "I'm not exactly certain that I know what the trouble is."

"Has it got to do with Michael?" prodded Mrs. Drake, admiring Mona's slow, tantalizing approach to the inevitable confession.

For a second Mona studied her friend cautiously, because she was still not positive to what extent Bea could be trusted. Would everything she said go right back to the Senator? Could she trust her to silence? Mona had an instinctive revulsion against sharing her personal problems with others (except Michael, only he never seemed to want to hear them) even though most of their friends in Georgetown were addicted to discussing intimate details about even weekend pickups they found in bars on Wisconsin Avenue. She hated the way, after downing a few Martinis at a party, those divulging friends of theirs would begin to tell what they did in bed together, or that they had just had a fight over nothing. She had come to the conclusion that most people have a compulsion to confess, to spill out their innermost problems to anyone who might listen. She always felt, too, that not only did they need to confess, but they expected you to assume the responsibility for what they had brought you in on. Now it was no longer *their* worry, it was *yours* too. Yet, if she did not trust Bea, who else was there to turn to? She could no longer hold in her frustrations, her nagging suspicions. She realized in desperation that she had come to the point in her life where she had to find someone to confide in or she would begin to act and say foolish things to everyone. If I could just clear out all the bubbling worries foaming about in my mind. After all, the mind must be able to hold only just so many at one time. If I could just–

"Well?" interrupted Mrs. Drake, who was tired of watching the obvious indecision on Mona's face.

"Yes, it has to do with Michael." She wanted to quickly get the whole problem out in the open and then forgotten.

"Not another woman?" guessed Mrs. Drake.

"No," remarked Mona angrily. "At least I don't think so. A wife would know that, wouldn't she? I mean sense it?"

"Some wives do," admitted Beatrice Drake. "You would, I'm sure. You've got a feminine mind, Mona. If it isn't a woman, what is it?"

"I wish I knew." She leaned forward. "I've asked Michael over and over again. Each time he refuses to discuss it. He simply walks away. Or ignores me. Everything seems to have gone flat between us. Like ginger ale does."

"Oh dear!" sighed Mrs. Drake. Monotony! The most deadly of all diseases that affect the institution of marriage. Very few survive it. And the worst part of the disease is that the victims don't even know they're infected until it's far too late. She knew from personal experience. "Tell me about it, dear."

"There's very little to tell really," said Mona, her throat choked with suppressed feelings. "You just suddenly wake up one morning and you find that a flatness has sprung up between you. Somehow, life together has become one-dimensional again. Like it was before you fell into love. The romance and mystery has evaporated. Now there is only routine."

This is much worse than I had ever suspected, thought Mrs. Drake. "But you both seem so happy together."

"Couldn't you feel the strain between us?" asked Mona, recalling that entire evening. He had gone to bed immediately after dinner, leaving her sitting alone in the living room.

"Are you sure, Mona? You couldn't just be imagining things? Sometimes we do imagine things just so life doesn't become too stale. Have you tried discussing what you feel with Michael?"

"Oh yes," she said cynically. "At least I've tried to. I told you, he simply gets up and walks away. Or he reads his newspaper. Sometimes I even feel he hates me. What can I do, Bea? Is it all gone? Down the drain? We were so happy."

We were so happy! There was the clue, the germ, the death knell. Mona was already talking in the *past* tense. Mrs. Drake had decided long ago that whenever the past tense arrived in the midst of a relationship there were two choices available. Either you buried the dead romance with ritualistic solemnity, storing away all pleasant reminders with moth balls of memory in order to preserve them for old age, or you could frantically erase every little poisonous hope that had gone into the marriage when it was alive and standing on its own two feet, you could deny that you were seriously in love in the first place. The other possibility is a more deadly one. If you were a man or woman bent on revenge, you deliberately inflated the corpse of the marriage with a willful denial that anything's wrong. This keeps the corpse from decomposing. In other words, you simply make living together a wake, with each one sitting across from the other at breakfast, having carefully put the dead marriage out of sight so it won't be in the way of the mourners.

"No," mused Mrs. Drake out loud. "A woman's always better."

"What do you mean?" asked Mona, her face cramped with puzzlement.

"Forgive me," laughed Mrs. Drake. "I was just thinking out loud. But a woman *is* always better. At least one of the marriage partners gets out alive. They both don't go sinking down into that horrible oblivion of quiet second-rate sentimentality known as duty to themselves and to their children. Why don't you try the last rite of vacationing together?" suggested Mrs. Drake. "That old insulin shot which proves either to convulse the patient back into the thick of life or send it merrily on its way to the elephants' graveyard."

"You seem so calloused about marriage," said Mona hastily.

"Do I?" Mrs. Drake reached across the table to squeeze her friend's hand maternally. "I didn't mean to sound that way, Mona. I've never mentioned this to you before, but I had already sent two marriages to that graveyard before I stumbled on the Senator. The first time I said, 'I do,' I believed I did. The second time I wasn't positive. The third time, well, the third time I decided I'd just take pot luck."

"That's very funny," said Mona. "I mean, I never had the least idea that you had been married to anyone but the Senator. You both seem so right for each other. So perfectly suited. You seem to understand him so well."

"You only learn that from experience," said Mrs. Drake humorously. "I don't like to talk about my other marriages because people begin to suspect that there's something wrong with me."

"Suspect you of what?"

"They begin to suspect that you're like a business that keeps running into bankruptcy. They suspect it's under bad management. And in my case it wasn't so. My choice of partners was unfortunate. But the management was in perfect shape."

"But what can I do?" cried out Mona exasperatedly. "I refuse to just stand by and do nothing about it."

"My dear," laughed Mrs. Drake, "you remind me of a friend of mine who was a little late in getting down to the pier to see a friend off. By the time she got there, she could just make out the stern of the liner disappearing in the distance. But in order to make herself feel better she began to wave her handkerchief and cried bucketfuls of tears just the same."

"Are you implying that it's too late for me to do anything?" She dared her friend with her eyes to say yes.

"Mona," exclaimed Mrs. Drake sitting back in her chair placidly, "the main trouble with marriage in America today is that the participants struggle too hard at making it a success. They act like it's one of those do-it-yourself-kit things. All the little pieces have to fit in properly or it's back to the store where it came from. If what you say is true about you and Michael, then I don't see that you can *do* anything. Everything's been *done*. People aren't clocks. You can't just turn a key and expect Michael to start keeping time again."

"I don't understand you," defended Mona. "Are you making fun of me?"

Mrs. Drake saw it was useless. "Forgive me, dear," she smiled over at her. "I suppose I did sound like I was making fun of you. And me too, and all the rest of us. If I don't make fun sometimes I think I would break down and cry for a year. Life can get too sad and depressing. We strive for just a crumb of happiness, something to hold on to, but we never seem to find it, unless we find it right in ourselves. That's why I make fun. Every now and then I make fun. After all, isn't my marriage with the Senator one of the funniest relationships you've ever seen?"

Oh Lord, thought Mona, she's going to get maudlin. She remembered perfectly the one or two Christmas Eves ago when Bea had broken down, crying like a baby. "Please," Mona called out to one of the waitresses passing by, "Could we order a cocktail?"

"Yes, a nice cool double Martini for me," mumbled Mrs. Drake, poking about in her purse for a handkerchief. She sniffled dangerously but held back any tears.

Mona suddenly had a silly desire to laugh. For the first time in all the years that they had been having lunch together she had felt the urge to confess to Bea, had wanted more than anything else to feel blatantly sorry for herself, to be able to pull out her handkerchief and have a good public cry. But Bea was beating her to it. She was right back where she was before she came in. I'll simply have to learn how to steel myself against Michael's odd behavior. That's what it was and nothing more. He was simply irritated and overworked. They hadn't had a good vacation in over three years. Another woman? How ridiculous. How could Bea think such a thing. She didn't know Michael.

"Mona," interrupted Mrs. Drake, blowing her nose gracefully, "I forgot to tell you, but there's a wonderful foreign movie up the street at the Dupont. We must go. It's about a lot of Italian peasants trying to push something or other up a hill. You know how those foreign films are. They're always trying to push something up or down to somewhere else. And they keep saying that Americans are restless."

Chapter Nine

The afternoon sun shone with such clear, clean brilliancy, cutting into shadows sharply, making curves and angles of rooftops and houses distinct, that Anna could no longer restrain herself. She had to go out for a walk. The sun drew her out like warmth draws out soreness in the flesh. Anna felt defenseless against it. The dazzling sunlight split the day apart as if there had been invisible doors, inviting Anna into it with promises of the perhapses, the maybes, the infinite possibilities of an adventure and exploration. As she walked along the green-coated pavements of Georgetown, the musty smell of wetness, of antiquity, of many past autumnal leaves assailed her nostrils, causing her to smile appreciatively at the deliciousness of objects, of twisting trees, of leaves jagged and transparent shaking gaily on the branches overhead.

The beauty of the world made war against her puritan senses, pulling, plucking, tugging at her sightless eyes, her soundless ears, her nose, her mouth, her tender skin, until like little eddies of water munching against a sand bank, particles of her resistance crumbled gently, soundlessly, flowing swiftly into the current of aliveness, of immediacy, of being herself in a lovely world. Impulsively she offered herself to life as she had to Christ, entirely. She smiled repeatedly as if she were practicing an exercise she had all but forgotten. The soreness, the crampedness left her caged-in self, and like a bird, newly released from its cage, soared high into the blueness overhead, searching frantically for the godhead of the sun.

* * *

"But of course you must realize," went on the general with the unflattering bushy moustache, "that the Gargon case is of utmost importance to the department. We must take every precaution to win it."

Inwardly, Michael Humphrey sighed. His hand held a yellow pencil which, all by itself, seemed to be drawing odd-shaped designs on the pad in front of him, reserved, he knew, for brilliant intuitive flashes that lawyers sometimes experienced. General de Witt had been talking for well over half an hour, and most of what he had been saying was absurd. Of course they had to win the case. Any fool could see that. He hadn't been working on it all these months in order to lose it. De Witt was simply giving them another Army pep talk before the game. He was positive that the client on the other side was saying the exact same thing to his lawyer. You have to win. Hell, thought Michael Humphrey, I'm bored with winning. I'm just as bored with losing. There must be a neutral ground somewhere. There must be a shady brook where humanity could rest and push aside the eternal struggle in the world to win or lose. Hadn't mankind come that far yet? Didn't it deserve just a few hours of rest before pushing on into oblivion?

"Now I'm not telling you this to disturb you fellows," said the general, lighting up a cigar. "But I just want you to be aware of hidden possibilities."

"We're quite aware of them," Michael said aloud, recklessly in fact, for he could tell by the general's raised eyebrow that his remark had disconcerted him. Is he being insolent? the general must be thinking. Or is he trying to side with me? Michael methodically drew a square, then with the point of the pencil he made a round, firm dot in the middle. That's me, he thought. That's my position in life.

"I think that will be all for the moment, gentlemen," said the officer, standing up abruptly.

Ah, Michael sighed with relief. The pep talk was over with. As he neatly shuffled his papers together and stacked them carefully in his briefcase, he was aware that General de Witt was watching him from the doorway. As he snapped the lock shut and started to push his chair back, the bulky presence of the general blocked him from moving.

"Michael," said the general in a serious tone, "are you taking a vacation this year?"

"A vacation?"

"You've been working pretty hard on this case." The seriousness changed to outright solicitude. "I don't know if I have the right to say this or not, but you seem so preoccupied lately. So self-absorbed."

"Really," he said lightly.

"I'm not the only one to notice this preoccupation, you understand," he said pleasantly.

Michael had visions of the other men discussing his behavior among themselves before he had come into the conference room. "Well," he said casually, "I guess I might have overworked myself lately."

"I knew it," smiled the officer happily. He put a friendly hand on Michael's shoulder and squeezed it. "As soon as this case is over, Michael, I'm gong to insist that you and Mona take a trip somewhere. Bermuda perhaps. The beaches are nice there this time of year."

"Yes," he said quietly. "Yes, maybe we should go." Michael could see the concern on the general's face changing to boisterous relief.

"I'll see you in court on Monday," he said, scratching his moustache.

"Yes," remarked Michael absentmindedly. "On Monday." Left alone in the conference room, he felt very disturbed,

disturbed mostly by the realization that the feelings he had been experiencing and thought secret, were not. He had not hidden them from anyone. They apparently knew or suspected that something was wrong with him. He had not been remotely successful nor as clever as he had imagined all these weeks. His dilemma was obvious even to such an insensitive personality as General de Witt's.

As he walked along the endless corridors of the Pentagon, then finally out the main doorway, he surveyed with trepidation the spider web of buildings that made Washington the sprawling city it was. He hesitated about signaling the car that had brought him, for the realization that his unusual behavior was so easily discernable made him want to evade even Joe Casey, the driver, who had been driving him for several years. In fact, as he glanced out over the glittering city, he felt resentful. Hell, all Washington must have noticed my behavior by now. But what could he do about it? He saw Joe Casey signal with his hand. As the car pulled up, he stepped inside. Cautiously he pushed himself back against the seat just in case someone should recognize him.

"Where to, Mr. Humphrey?" asked the driver.

Anywhere, he wanted to say, but Washington. Instead, he asked to be driven back to his office.

* * *

Like one intoxicated from a gentle wine, Anna stood now, smiling secretly at her inner pleasure, watching the busy world of Georgetown whirl around her, for she had traveled the myriad streets, up and down, in and out, like a young, panting huntress, surveying the scene cautiously, and hoping against hope that luck might be with her again, and she would see the man she had met in Dumbarton Oaks. Several times she had wanted to hurry back to the park, but either out of fear of disappointment or out of embarrassment if he actually should be there, she had taken a third resolution, to remain in the confines of the business district. Now, however, she saw that it was after three. Her afternoon was rapidly running out. If she was going to the park she had to go now.

What if he should be there? She argued with herself conscientiously. There would be no reason for him to suspect she had come deliberately. After all, if he just should be there, who knows, perhaps he too had returned to find her. But her fears were needless. He was nowhere in sight. Two old ladies struggled together up one of the graveled paths, a nurse with a child sat dreamily in the shade, but no one else.

Anna sat down on one of the benches and watched a gardener pruning the bushes. He pruned with such care and consideration that she could tell how much the planting meant to him. Everyone seems to have someone or something to love except me. Only I seem shut out or off from loving. As she bent over to pick up a dried, wrinkled leaf that had just fallen from the tree overhead, she recalled a scene that had happened (Could it have been just a week ago?) when she had been sitting alone out in the convent yard, had been in fact, stooping over to pick up another leaf, when she was aware of the presence of Sister Mary Francis watching her from a distance. She stood there silently, eyes sad and face gentle, hands reaching out to touch, to offer consolation, gestures meaningful, warm, but no words spoken. Then finally she walked towards Anna, sitting down slowly next to her.

"I know there are no words, Anna," she said finally, low and regretfully, "to offer you at a time like this. When I try to imaging myself in your place I become panicky and afraid. I couldn't imagine what I would do if I wouldn't know where to go or what to do. I would spend the rest of my life aimlessly searching for what I had lost." She stopped, smiled encouragingly then patted her hand. "But with you it will be different. With you God knows what He is doing. You are full of love, bursting with it like a plum that is over-ripe. You would grow too full of pain if you stayed here. Love in you is spontaneous and unfettered. The love I have for God is different. My love seems controlled and channeled. I am continually afraid that it will get out of hand and if it should do that, I know I would be ruined. But you would wither under the conditions here in the convent. Now you've got the whole world to love. The people in it must be starved for love. So be generous. Be unafraid."

Be generous. Be unafraid. The words echoed lightly in Anna's ears now. The sweet, delicate presence of the nun remained like a fragrance in her memory. Anna was back with the leaf in her hand. By this time the two old ladies had disappeared, the nurses gone, but the gardener, prodding lovingly at the earth was still there. Be generous. Be unafraid. But what Sister Mary Francis apparently didn't know was that even though an awful lot of human beings wanted love, they seemed too afraid to reach out for it. Who knows? Maybe they, too, wanted to be generous and unafraid. But who would be the first to admit it? Who would dare? She closed her eyes, fighting back bitter tears of resentment. Didn't anyone need her. Anyone? Anywhere?

* * *

The whole thing happened so rapidly that Michael Humphrey had difficulty later in remembering exactly what occurred before the accident, but he was never able to forget as long as he lived what came after it.

The driver had just mentioned the fact that the weather was unusually hot for this time of year. Michael was going to contradict him because Washington had known many freakish warm days even as early as February. However, he refrained.

Instead, he reached inside his pocket and took out a package of cigarettes. As he pulled one out for himself, in a sudden impulse of generosity, he leaned forward to offer Joe Casey one. It was in that instant that he saw the child dart off the pavement away from the person beside it, and before the car in front could stop, there was a dull thump, then the screech of brakes being put on. His driver was just able to stop short of the car in front. From the sidewalk came a scream that rang and rang in Michael's ears for many days after.

For several moments Michael sat rigid in the back because the shock of seeing the accident seemed to have momentarily paralyzed him. His driver, however, jumped out immediately and ran up towards the man who was stumbling out of the car that had hit the child. Michael could tell from the frightened expression on both their faces that the child was dead. He reached for the handle of the door, opened it, then stood out on the street watching. He saw the unfortunate driver bend over, seeing him move as if life had suddenly slowed down, action retarded like in a film, watched him straighten up again, only in his arms he held a limp little body, the head dangled loosely to one side, and as the driver turned towards the figure on the sidewalk, Michael walked towards them as if hypnotized.

The mother stood there defenselessly watching the man approaching with his dreadful burden being offered to her as if the child might have been a bag full of oranges that had carelessly slipped out of her arms, which he was returning politely, perhaps even expecting a smile of thanks, a kind word, only when Michael stared openly in the woman's face, there was on it such a deep, heartbreaking expression of the hopelessness of the situation. The man actually knelt down on the edge of the sidewalk, apparently no longer able to watch her heart-rending struggle as she reached out for her son, a second ago alive and laughing, now dead and silent, but his head bowed, Michael could hear him saying incoherently, "Forgive me ... forgive me ... forgive me." Over and over he mumbled the same words.

Deep within Michael, like a bubble rising up from a deep well, came an enormous, overwhelming sense of tragedy, enveloping him in its intensity, until he found himself shaken with sobs deep and uncontrollable. In some way he did not understand, he was experiencing the feelings that he imagined the mother of the child must be feeling, and in this grief, now exposed, all the frustrations that he had been suppressing in the last two years, like a newly opened wound, oozed out bright red blood. Her tragedy had the effect of lancing his own festering inflammation, making him incapable of actually noticing what was happening around him.

How long he stood out on the road he did not remember. When he looked up again there was a semi-circle of faces, staring, babbling, surmising, until one of them, a man, leaned towards him to ask if he felt all right. Only then did he realize in what a dazed state he had been. He looked embarrassingly about for Joe Casey. A policeman was interrogating him. Traffic had all but stopped on the bridge. Frantically he looked around for the unfortunate driver. He was surrounded by three officers with his hat off in his hand. He talked incoherently. Then Michael searched for the mother. Not too far away was another huddled group of people, and slowly, fearfully he made his way in that direction.

As he came towards the huddled group of dulled silence, the group, as if instinctively sensing his presence, parted to let him view the mother sitting on the side of the bridge with the lifeless mess of clothes and flesh, holding her little boy close, hugging him against all human effort to bring him back to life again, knowing full well the impossibility of it all, the unfairness, the senselessness, the pointlessness, which could never be explained to herself nor to the father, who must be off somewhere working, secure in the idea of seeing both his wife and child at the end of the day.

Michael felt an emotional urge to say something to the woman. But what was there for him to say? What possible gesture could he make? There in her arms, bleeding and still, was the result of fate. None of them could rearrange it. There was no one to whom they could appeal for justice. Fate was done. It lay there between them. In what he considered the most impunitive remark he could possibly make, he leaned forward, and in a choked voice intended only for the two of them, or maybe the three, he said, "I'm very sorry."

She glanced up into his face uncomprehendingly as if she had never seen him before. In fact, he realized that she had not even noticed that there was even a car behind the car that had struck her little boy. There was nothing, he realized then, that could pierce agonizing grief. Her grief was so great that it made comprehension impossible. Her grief probably prevented her from losing her mind or going into physical shock. Suppose, he thought suddenly, it had been our car that had struck the child. How would he have felt then?

He was tapped on his shoulder. A policeman was at his side with a writing pad. As he gave him all the information he asked for, he was aware in the background of the thin whine of a siren as an ambulance sped around the Lincoln Memorial in their direction. Out of respect for the situation, Michael noticed that the policeman refrained from questioning him any further while the doctor jumped out of the back of the ambulance to take the mother's burden from her arms, a burden which she refused to relinquish, so both of them were placed in the back of the car. Once the car had left, the crowd dispersed. Traffic began to flow again. Only the two cars were left. And in front of the first one was a dark stain.

Looking scared and friendless, Michael heard the driver of the first car saying, "What do you want me to do now?"

"You'll have to come to the station with us, Mr. Riley," said one of the officers matter-of-factly.

"May I go in your car?" he asked uneasily.

"You're free to go now, Mr. Humphrey," said the policeman at his side. "We'll probably need you for a witness. We'll notify you."

Michael wanted to ask if he could go in their car too, but when he saw the forlorn expression of Joe Casey's face, he knew he could not let him down.

As they drove away from the remaining automobile neither one of them spoke. Just after they reached Constitution Avenue, the driver said, "Gosh, it's so hard to believe. One minute we're driving along talking, then the next minute a little boy runs out and gets killed. I can't take it in."

"Neither can I," admitted Michael Humphrey. For the first time in his life he was aware of how near death was. Right at your elbow. Breathing down your neck. But the average person is shielded from it. Protected and coddled. To them death is usually the liberation from a painful illness. Never sudden and shocking. Never unprepared for. That child is dead, he kept repeating to himself, when only a few minutes ago he was alive. That was death I saw happening. Again, before his eyes came the mother's uncomprehending expression when she saw her little boy in the driver's arms being offered to her silently. Again in his ears came the piercing scream right after the thump. Michael closed his eyes. He felt sick. "Casey," he said hurriedly, "I think you'd better let me out here. I need a little air."

"Yes, sir." Casey understood. He pulled to the side.

As Michael walked along the pavement, he realized he had been thoroughly frightened. He was trembling in fact. But more than anything else, he was astonished by the awareness that he had finally felt something deeply enough, deeply enough to make him cry, to make him care, to make him afraid. Oh God, he thought desperately, it's taken death to show me what life is.

And what a fool I've been. He walked for over an hour then finally he hurried in the direction of Georgetown.

Chapter Ten

Anna could tell by the way the sunlight filtered through the leaves in the trees around her that the afternoon had fled. He had not come. Even the gardener had left. Only a rake lay flat on the grass as a reminder that he had been there. She stood up and began walking aimlessly along the paths, marveling at the beauty of the flowerbeds bursting with tulip leaves and thin pointy ones she knew to be jonquils. As she bent over to touch a tissue-thin blue crocus she was aware that there was someone standing over by the entrance watching her.

She stood up, shaded her eyes, for the sun flickered directly into them, and with a quick intake of breath she stood motionless waiting for him to move.

As he came towards her she realized instantly that something was the matter. Perhaps it was the way he moved, disjointedly as if were rushing haphazardly towards a final destination, but as he came closer she saw disturbance clearly on his face, in his eyes, blurred and large with fear.

"I thought," he began breathlessly, standing before her with both hands out in a suppliant gesture, "I thought.... I hoped that you might be here." He stumbled backwards as if he needed support.

She quickly held out her arm, then searched for a nearby bench. "Let's go over there," she suggested, nodding her head to the left. Obediently he followed her.

"Something awful just happened," he began again, not waiting any longer, unable to control himself or to hold in what he had just been through. "This little boy...." he said breathlessly. "We were driving over the Memorial Bridge when this little boy...." But he covered his face with his hand as if to block out of sight the picture he wanted to talk about.

"Sit here," she said gently, forcing him down on the bench. "Try not to talk," she suggested. "I think you'd feel better if you didn't."

He plunged his left hand into his pocket, took out a handkerchief, then wiped his eyes roughly, blotting up the tears that had begun again. "I just came from an accident," he said, determined to get it all out this time.

"An accident?" she cried out, thinking he had been the one.

He took a deep breath. "We saw a little boy run over," he said with great effort. "On Memorial Bridge." He glanced fearfully over into her eyes to see what effect this would have on her. "The car in front of us killed him." He saw only solicitude and deep concern.

"Killed him?" she repeated in a whisper.

He nodded his head, bit brutally into his lips to keep from crying again, then banged his fist down on the wooden bench. "One minute alive, then...." The thought of it forced him to stand up and walk about nervously. "It wasn't even the driver's fault," he continued. "This little boy just ran out on the road. The driver didn't have a chance to stop. I saw the whole thing happen." He stopped to look straight into her face. "I saw the expression on the mother's face when the driver handed her back her little dead son. I've never seen such a look on any human being's face before. That pathetic expression. No protest. Just sudden resignation." Suddenly an echo of the scream that followed pierced his ears. He flung his hands over them as if to stifle the sound within.

"Don't. Don't," Anna cried, jumping up. "You're just tormenting yourself. You've got to forget about it." She tried pulling him back down on the bench so he could collect himself better. "Just try and forget."

"But I don't want to forget it," he insisted angrily. "I want to remember all of it. Nothing has affected me like this for years. No, I don't ever want to forget that woman's face. I actually felt something then. Something inside of me."

Tears filled her eyes suddenly. "Please," she begged him, "stop tormenting yourself like this."

"There was something about the way that woman looked that had a meaning for me." His red eyes looked perplexed and uncertain. "Her agony made me feel a part of something larger than myself. I can't explain it yet, but I no longer feel alone."

"Please," she begged.

"I'll tell you something else," he said, looking straight into her eyes. "God was there. I felt Him. I swear I felt Him."

Anna did not understand exactly what he meant at first, because she did not know him well enough to be familiar with his behavior, but she senses from what he had been telling her that he had a need to enlarge or blow up this accident into proportions beyond reason. There was some inner compulsion for him to suffer, to torment himself, to identify with the mother's sorrow. But when he said that God was there, she was affronted. "You should not bring God into this," she said firmly.

Her remark irritated him. "And why not?" he asked angrily. "Does He just belong to you?"

Anna's cheek burned with resentment. She stood up as if she no longer desired to sit next to him. "I mean, when you're upset and irrational like you are now, you should leave God out of it," she explained. "Later you will be able to see the accident clearer. You'll see that God had nothing whatever to do with it."

"But," he said, aggravated by her self-righteousness, "I *know* He was there. I felt Him. I can't explain it too well but it seemed to as if suddenly there was nothing existing except that woman, the man with the dead child, and me."

"And what happened to God?"

"God was the over-all feeling," he explained. "He was all of us and more. I'll never forget that sensation. I guess I would have to call it a religious sensation. But I've never experienced anything more real in my life." He looked up at her. "Don't you understand what I mean? Didn't you just come out of a convent? Isn't that what you were doing there? Trying to experience God?"

This time she felt he had gone too far. His behavior was becoming more frantic, more irrational and certainly more absurd. She could hardly believe that he was the same man that she had met a few days ago. "Why did you come here hunting for me?" she asked.

"Because I thought you would understand," he said earnestly. "You said you had just come from a convent. And you asked me if there was something you could do to help me," he reminded her.

Yes, she remembered she had. But how reckless can you be with generosity? "What can I do to help you?" she said, standing hesitantly before him.

"I need you," he said faintly. "I need you somehow. Only you seem to understand. There's something about you...."

Anna was unexpectedly frightened. Most of her life she had needed other people but this was the first time that someone openly admitted needing her. Was she capable of giving help to this man? Did she actually want to? "What kind of help?" she asked cautiously.

"You were right the other afternoon," he confessed. "Something is wrong with me. I'm not myself. I don't seem to have ever felt anything. I never have."

"Do you mean," she asked fearfully, "that you feel something for me?"

"Yes," he said, standing up. "Yes, I mean that. I don't know why but I haven't been able to forget you. I even went out to look for you later that afternoon." He looked at her helplessly. "Then when the accident occurred and I felt this presence of God so near, I knew that I had to find you. I thought maybe you might be able to explain it."

His words hung in the air, then quickly fell into nothingness. Yes, she could see that he meant what he was saying ... and thank goodness he did not suspect that she was there for that very same reason. For that she was grateful. She would never tell him now. "What's your name?" she asked softly.

He hesitated. "Michael," he said with difficulty. "Michael Humphrey."

She politely told him hers. "Why don't we sit down again," she suggested, smiling slightly as if to encourage him.

"You don't have to, you know," he reminded her.

"You mean," she said pleasantly, "don't have to help you?"

"Yes," he replied feebly, feeling suddenly that she was going to refuse.

Anna sat quietly for a minute or two, watching him, absorbing as much as she could of his appearance, of the way his black hair curled slightly in the back, and how straight his nose seemed to be. Her eyes took in as much as she dared without seeming to be rude. Yes, she thought, somehow, in some way that I haven't been aware of, I have fallen in love with this man. The realization seemed incredible to her. Only last week she was full of sadness like a widow bereaved and now one week later she felt joy in her heart. She had to repress the strongest urge to reach out and lock her hand in his. Hadn't he admitted that he felt something for her? Hadn't he? "Mr. Humphrey," she stammered awkwardly, "I will be very pleased to see you whenever you like. I think I told you that I am staying with my grandmother, Mrs. Leighton Ross, over on P Street. If there is anything that I can do to help you...."

Before she could finish, he had reached out and taken her

hand in gratitude. "You mean we can see each other again?" The very idea of it made him feel less disturbed, for there was so much he wanted to ask about herself, about the convent, about religious life, but mostly about her religious feelings. And what, most of all, was a vocation? Confronted like he had just been by death, he realized that he could no longer go on letting his life drift aimlessly, killing the minutes, hours and days the way he had been doing, that now, immediately, he had to make life count again, make his feelings come alive that had been dormant most of his life. Death had shown him how thin the life line was, how quickly it could be snapped, and with this realization came panic. He could postpone the inevitable no longer. He had deliberately anchored himself in marriage, in Mona, in the children, but now he realized that he could never do that again. He had to find something stronger than that to hold him. With the awareness of death breathing down his neck, he knew he had to find help, relief, and he felt that only this woman could show him where it could be found. He was far too preoccupied to notice that she had slowly removed her hand from his, that her face was flushed and her mouth opened slightly, as if his touch had converted her completely.

"I must be going," she said reluctantly.

"But we will see each other again?" he reiterated, fearing that she might disappear once more.

"Yes," she nodded her head. "I would be very pleased to."

"Maybe," he said urgently, "maybe we could see each other on Saturday. We could have lunch together. We could talk."

"That would be very nice," she said. "Only, are you certain of your feelings for me?"

"But yes," he replied, with a smile on his lips. "Didn't I just tell you that I came back here to find you?"

"All right then," she said, as they started to walk up the path. Yet, inside she was confused. There was something she did not quite understand about him, about his feelings for her. But that could wait until Saturday.

He suddenly realized that perhaps it might be a good idea to mention that he was married and where he lived. But he decided that for once in his life he wanted a friend that was his alone. They both could talk more freely. "Shall I walk you home?" he asked.

She nodded her head. She was very pleased to see that he was no longer that frantic, disturbed person that had come stumbling into the park. Already he seemed more assured of himself. I wonder, she thought, if I have already given him that much comfort?

Together they walked out of Dumbarton Oaks. Each one was wondering what the other might be thinking but both were very far from the truth.

Chapter Eleven

If he took one more drink, Mona Humphrey thought she would scream. He had come home very agitated but when she questioned him he had told her disinterestedly that there had been an accident that afternoon coming over Memorial Bridge on the way back from the Pentagon.

"Oh Michael!" she had cried out with concern, for however lightly he talked of it, he was, at last *sharing* something with her. From the manner in which he said it, moving towards the kitchen for a drink, she naturally assumed that perhaps a fender was bent or a bumper pushed in. Then they had chatted about this and that, even that she had had her periodic lunch with Beatrice Drake, while her eyes followed him back and forth, one frantic highball after another, yet he remained cool, distant but polite, the entire time. Then her thoughts wandered back to the accident. "Will you have to go to court? " she asked, picking haphazardly at one of the pillows on the couch.

"I imagine so," he said distinctly. "You see, I saw the boy killed right in front of me."

Mona stared at him for a second as if he might be kidding. He seemed so unconcerned, so above the situation. "You saw him killed right in front of you...."

He nodded his head matter-of-factly, took another swallow of his highball, turned about in his chair, and, as if he had an added thought, he said, "I saw the driver pick him up and take him over to the mother, who was waiting on the sidewalk."

"How dreadful," she said.

"I can't forget that woman's face," he said, staring down at his drink.

"Why, that must have been an awful experience for you," she said, full of concern.

"Does it disturb you just hearing about it?" he asked, studying her face closely.

"Of course it disturbs me," she said, sitting down again. "If it disturbs you it naturally disturbs me."

"I see," he said.

And he was terribly disturbed. Mona could see that. Why else was he drinking one highball after another? Why else was he trying to remain coldly objective about what he had seen? She had the feeling that he was trying very hard to behave like a guest at a dinner party, being polite, yet disinterested, kind but indifferent. "Michael...." she said with a great deal of feeling, hoping for once that they would not remain apart, hiding honest feelings from each other. "Don't shut me out. Please don't."

For a second his gaze faltered, his hand trembled enough to force him to sit his drink down. "Shut you out?" he repeated. "Mona, you and I have been as far apart as the sun is from the moon. Let's be honest. Admit it. Even the death of a little boy couldn't bring us back together again."

She was stunned. She reached helplessly out for support, holding on to the side of the sofa. This was the first time that he had ever voiced his opinion about their relationship. Now that he had, she sensed disaster, only she refrained from putting too much credibility into what he had said. Somewhere in the back of her mind she understood that something was happening to her husband, that something had begun to unravel which she was powerless to stop. Yes, like Bea had said about that friend of hers, she felt like she was seeing her husband off on a voyage and all that she could do was stand on the pier and wave good-bye. She was benumbed by the actuality of it. Suddenly inside she was overwhelmed with fear for the possibility that he might not return. "Michael?" she called out in a trembling voice, hoping against hope that at the last minute he might jump overboard and swim back to shore, back into her sheltering arms. "Do you hear me, Michael?" But he went on staring vacantly at the newspaper, showing by no expression whatsoever that he had even been aware that she had spoken.

I don't believe it, she kept telling herself in desperation. This just can't be happening to our marriage. We've both put so much into it. We've worked so hard at the relationship. And now, like the many-angulated pieces of a jigsaw puzzle, the picture was falling apart and she knew that in a hundred years she would never be able to fit the pieces back into their proper places again. How much of it was her fault? If she were going to be honest, just exactly how much had she contributed to this gradual estrangement?

Hadn't she known from the very beginning that Michael was not in love with her? Hadn't she known it yet pretended not to care? He liked her, was even sentimentally fond of her, but he had never really been in love with her. In many ways he had used her as a convenience, as an easy way out of his own personal dilemma, a dilemma of fear and loneliness, had married her because she had, in the end, insisted that they do so. (She had thought him too shy to broach the subject.) Day after day she had waited patiently for him to fall in love with her, only that miracle never seemed to have occurred. Finally, one day, in despair, wasn't her mother getting impatient with Michael for wasting her daughter's good years, she had deliberately forced the issue by saying, "Michael, marry me right away." He had not refused. At the time she had thought his acquiescence the beginning of love, now she realized that he had not even cared enough to refuse. He had, which was characteristic of him, simply accepted the situation. And in the end, wasn't it her efforts that had made the marriage what it was?

She smiled painfully to herself as she went quickly over these facts. Whatever their marriage had been she had given it the energy, the tone, the meaning. He had been her blackboard. She wrote the symbols, the directions, only now, after so many years of living together, the symbols had rubbed off in the living. The entire relationship of husband and wife must have been hopeless from the beginning. What they had begun with, they were ending with. Her persistent love for him, his apparent indifference to her. Suddenly she wanted to be angry, to hate him openly, to scream, to do anything that would destroy his selfish complacency. Hadn't she the right to protest? Yet in the end, all she found herself doing was sitting there watching how oddly the smoke from his cigarette curled like a rope twisting in mid air.

What protestation could she make? By asking him to marry her hadn't she tied her own hands? By asking him like she had, ("Mother, I don't think I should ask him." "Don't be a fool, Mona! Michael would never think of asking any woman to marry him. He hasn't got that much self-assurance.") hadn't she ended her own self-respect? Yes, she could see it all now, laid out before her like a table map. Their married life twisted and turned like a river, until it gradually ended by wiggling into a small thin line, a stagnant stream. Weren't there high mountains scattered about? Hadn't they avoided those completely? But that was it, of course. They had stayed down in the valleys, in the peaceful plateaus. The atmosphere on the mountain tops would have made them short of breath. Yes, now she could understand it. She had placed herself in that dangerous, unfair position of always being abandoned. Having children had not helped. Hadn't she used them as blackmail to hold him closer, to bind him to her with added responsibilities, only, and this pained her more than all the rest, wasn't he even more indifferent to them than he had ever been to her?

Impulsively she stood up, went over to his chair, knelt down on the floor and touched his arm like a little girl trying to distract her parent from a concentration that did not include her. "Michael, look at me." She said it forcefully as if he had to look, as if she would remain there on the floor for the rest of her life if he did not obey. Again, another sort of blackmail. When she looked into his eyes there was nothing there, no hatred, no resentfulness. Just a blankness, a refusal to admit that he knew what she was feeling. He had shut her out completely. She was too late to appeal.

"Did you want to say something?" he asked.

"What's going to happen...." she began, but she could not go on. Her eyes flooded with tears. She hated herself for weakening in front of him. "What's going to happen to us?"

He folded the paper carefully. "I don't know what's going to happen," he admitted honestly. "I personally feel that whatever we did have is ended. Time has moved on. We have nothing left for each other. It's out of our hands now." He smiled sadly. "Nothing's going to happen, Mona. Nothing has been happening to us for years." He stood up abruptly and went towards the kitchen for another drink.

Oh, God, she thought, could that be true? Maybe he might feel that way but she did not. Somehow their relationship with each other had not been right. There was something off key about it. He always seemed to be retreating while she spent the years advancing. They never had, from the very beginning, been able to communicate their personal thoughts and feelings to each other. ("Mother, he never tells me anything about himself." "Still waters run deep, dear. Give him time. You'll see. Mother knows.") She realized now that they had spent their whole married life living obliquely with each other, speaking veiled words, making furtive gestures, keeping always away from the truth that he was not in love with her and she was too much in love with him. Unevenly matched. This was the first time, as far back as she could remember, that they had ever been as honest as they were being right now. Too much anxiety would have ensued on both sides. Somehow they must have made a silent gentleman's agreement not to mention the truth about their marriage to each other. Even though she had never agreed verbally, she realized that she had been committed to keeping her personal needs to herself and letting him have his. They were so progressive, she had thought at the time. So modern. So clever.

Now, by saying, "What's going to happen to us?" hadn't she implied a contract, a partnership, a mutual feeling, a common wellspring of love which she knew had never existed? Hadn't she just placed both of them in a most embarrassing position?

As he came back into the room there was a frown on his face. Puzzlement was in his eyes. "Mona," he said with a faint smile on his lips, "even though I don't think anything is going to happen to us, that doesn't mean that there is no possibility of anything happening to each of us separately."

There, she thought nostalgically, he has just torn up the contract. "Separately?" she said blankly. "Yes, maybe separately." Only she knew deep inside that she wanted to be with him always. But she was relieved now. He had stated his position finally. She knew where she was. "I'll have to think about it," she said seriously. "You see…. I never thought … about you and me…." She waved her hand at him when he tried to speak. "Don't say any more please. Just let me alone. Please just let me alone." She watched him sit his glass down on the table, get up, and staggering slightly, she had not been aware that he had had so much to drink, he walked towards the front door. He hesitated. He did not turn around. Finally, he gripped the doorknob and opened it. He hesitated again. Then shut the door behind him.

The moment the door closed, a fragile sort of peace entered the room. She was still kneeling on the floor where he had been sitting. She closed her eyes for a second, then opened them again as if she were testing her aloneness. No, he was gone. She was surprised how relieved she felt to have him out of the house, and who knows, maybe, in the end, out of her life. Somehow she was dimly aware that he had been cramping her behavior as a human being for years. Perhaps when you married so early you never had the chance to develop into a more complete human being. Could proximity stunt development? Hadn't they both been unconsciously trying to salvage the self-respect they had lost long ago? Slowly she pulled herself up and walked woodenly towards the open doors. The night air was chilled but the touch of it on her warm skin made her feel more relaxed, more real. For a moment she pushed her troubles away, hanging them on top of the moon. Later she would decide what to do.

Chapter Twelve

"You seem so quiet this evening," Mrs. Ross said finally, for she had been knitting feverishly while her granddaughter sat across the way staring into the fire. There had been a chill in the air so Anna had begged for just one last fire before the weather became too warm. Now the little flames, like tongues, licked slowly up the sides of the logs, crackling and dancing, making golden reflections across Anna's intense and earnest face. "Is there something wrong?" She asked carefully.

Anna looked up, confused for the moment, because her grandmother had broken into the reverie she was enjoying. She had been back in Dumbarton Oaks, recalling vividly each thing that had happened, each word that had been spoken, each emotion that she had been aware of. "What did you say, grandmother?" She smiled charmingly, as if whatever it was, she could hardly wait to hear it.

Mrs. Ross looked troubled. "My dear," she said impatiently, putting her knitting to one side. "What has come over you this evening? You seem so preoccupied with yourself. Has something happened?"

Oh, if I could just tell her, Anna thought. I could just make her feel how happy I am. How excited I feel. But she was afraid to. She had felt this same reluctance years ago when she had first sensed the possibilities of a religious vocation. Her immediate reaction was to hide this awareness, to nurture it alone in secret, for she had that primitive feeling that once she brought her secret up into light, brought it out in conversation, there was the fearful possibility that the light might be too strong for such a tender plant, and shrivel up the leaves in a matter of minutes. Now the awareness that she was in love caused her to panic slightly. "No!" she said emphatically. "Nothing has happened. I think maybe I'm just beginning to realize that I'm free again, that I can feel and do what I want to now."

Ah, so that was it, thought Mrs. Ross with relief. The shock of being out of the convent was gradually wearing off. The possibilities of a future were beginning to assert themselves once again. "I'm glad to hear that," she said, nodding her head in approval. "I think maybe buying new clothes might have helped that along, don't you?"

Lord, thought Anna, I'd forgotten about that. Had he noticed how she looked there in the garden? Probably not. He was too worried about himself. But they were to see each other again Saturday. They were to have lunch. She couldn't imagine how she could wait that long. She would actually be sitting across from him. Maybe there would be music and a rose on the table. She jumped up suddenly, her face flushed and her eyes feverishly bright. "Grandmother." She could not bear hiding all of her happiness. "I'm so happy. So very happy." Surely that gave nothing away.

Her grandmother sat very still watching her. A log popped inconsiderately in the fireplace. "Anna?" She was about to interrogate her, for she realized now that something *had* happened to her granddaughter, and whatever had happened occurred from the time she had gone out for her walk until she returned for dinner. Hadn't she seen that vague, flushed, hypnotic expression on many a young girl's face? Indeed, hadn't she had it on her own several times? She knew instinctively that Anna was in love. But consideration restrained her from asking personal questions. She'll tell me about it when she wants to. Perhaps she wants to hug the feeling close before letting me know. She reached out, her rings sparkled gaily on her fingers from the firelight, and pulled her granddaughter down beside her on the couch. "You're a very sweet girl," she said proudly.

Tears sprung up instantly in Anna's eyes. She glanced with uncertainty into her grandmother's penetrating but understanding eyes, saw the wrinkles about her mouth, the chin firm and proud, the little nosegay pinned neatly on her dress, and in some way that she found difficult, Anna wanted to express how much the wholeness of her grandmother meant, but there were no words exactly to encompass what she wanted to say. There seemed to her no way to impart what she was feeling so deeply. Furtively she lifted her grandmother's hand and laid it gently against her cheek.

"Ah!" sighed Mrs. Ross softly, for she knew for certain. Anna was in love to overflowing.

Chapter Thirteen

After Mona had put the children to bed, she came downstairs, sighed deeply, and hesitated just as she was about to walk into the living room. With a tremendous thud, the realization that her marriage was about to end pounded into her awareness. She stood there, thunderstruck by the actuality of her situation. For the first time in her life she would actually have to admit that she had lost. Perhaps for this reason more than all the others, she began to hate Michael. He had made her lose. Hadn't they been involved in the game of marriage? Wasn't he simply refusing to hit the ball back this time? In fact, hadn't he walked straight off the field? How would she ever be able to face her mother, her friends, most of all herself, if she let the score stay as it was? Yet, what good did it do to win if your opponent didn't even care to play? No, Michael was winning by default and that wasn't even fair.

Like an athlete momentarily stunned, Mona gasped for air, slumped against the wall, and was just about ready herself to walk off the field when the stubborn side of her personality, the side that could rearrange reality to suit her own immediate needs, said no. Don't give in. Come back for more. Force him out into the open again. Have another round. For if she accepted the failure there was too much else she would have to begin accepting too. Within herself this acceptance would mean most of all having made the wrong decision in the first place by marrying Michael, and that she belligerently refused to do. She refused to let her illusions perish, even if single-handed she had to pump life back into the relationship. For if she didn't, what was left? There would be only cups and saucers. Only Georgetown, meaningless and futile without Michael. Only Bea to talk with. Only the children upstairs. Only the sound of birds chirping nonsense in the garden. "Damn it," she cried out. If he wants to destroy all of this then let him. But I won't. I won't lift one finger to let him go. He'll have to do it all on his own.

All on his own! The words danced before her eyes like a bulletin just off the wires. All on his own! Fear clutched violently at her throat, they sunk down into her stomach. Suppose...? But that would be impossible. But just suppose that he wasn't doing this on his own. That there *was* someone else. Just suppose that.... Just suppose.... Could Bea have known something that she didn't know? What was it? Was that why she had asked if there was another woman? Agitatedly she moved about the room, now ready for action. Suspicion was the only fuel she needed to ignite the flames of hate and resentment that were beginning to smolder inside her.

Michael and another woman? Was that the explanation then? She bit the back of her knuckles nervously. Maybe that was where he was right now. Telling her what had happened. But what could she do about it? She couldn't very well follow him when he left the house. But could that be where he went? Another woman at his side. Encouraging him to leave her. Giving him strength to act. Backing him in the undertaking. The coward, that's what he is. A coward. He couldn't come right out and tell the truth. All these weeks he had been acting so oddly. Avoiding her. Be patient with me, he had asked her. And God, how patient she had been. Afraid to move, to speak, to touch. Be patient with me, hell. I'm through being patient. I've got to do something. I can't just stand here. She thought of calling Bea but decided against it. She had already said far too much at lunch.

She hurried over to the telephone book and flung it open

roughly. In the back was the yellow section and her capable fingers flipped the pages until she found what she was hunting for. Detective agencies. But so many of them. Which one should she choose? There was one agency that said it was open twenty-four hours. She memorized the number, closed the book, then hurried back to the telephone. For a second she hesitated, wondering if what she was about to do was the best solution. But the idea that Michael might be with another woman at that very moment when she was going through so much hell alone spurred her on to dial. When the man's voice at the other end answered she leaned forward as if she were in a booth. "I'd like to make an appointment, please," she said softly, so that she could not be overheard by the children upstairs.

Chapter Fourteen

Was that yellow circle up there the moon? he wondered as he staggered up the street. The branches overhead cut across its surface like aged lines on a human face. "Old moon," he called out. "Go away, old moon. Let me alone. Let me alone." He had had far too much to drink and he knew it. But where was he to go now? What was he to do? He understood that everything was up between him and Mona. Ended. His little column of figures about himself had finally been added up and he had the total sticking inside his brain. 000. That was it. Now even Mona knew. And on top of it all, that sad, sad woman's face kept coming back. Her expression kept digging and digging into his memory. "Forgive me," he began to mumble. "Oh, please forgive me." Again and again he got himself confused with the driver of the other car.

The whiskey had loosened up his thoughts enough that his thinking had become frightfully clear. As clear and as bright as the moonlight that shivered on the treetops. He had reached the bitter end. That was it, wasn't it? He was trying to pour what was left of himself back into the cup he had been drinking out of most of his life. Only it no longer worked. The cup had leaked. "Oh, Mona," he sobbed, "I've made such a mess of things." His self-pity came like a tidal wave, engulfing him, pulling him down into the deepest, unhappiest part of himself. He staggered and almost fell. He gasped for air. I'm drowning, he thought resignedly. This is the end. How had he come to this? How? What went wrong? Who could save him?

He stumbled blindly forward and had to reach out for a wall to support him. He clutched onto it with both hands as if he were caressing it, then he pounded with his fists against the bricks, begging it to give way, to swallow him up. "Help me!" he cried out agonizingly. "Please.... Please, God, help me." There. There, he had said it. After all these years he had said it. Help me. Please God help me. In crying out for help he knew that he had torn away all the dreadful years of alienation, of wanting to stand alone, against life, against people, against himself, but most of all, against God.

"I *want* my miracle now," he cried out angrily. "I want it now." His knees gave way under him, or was he kneeling, and he sank to the pavement, still clutching onto the wall, breaking his fingernails until they bled. Then he passed out quietly.

Chapter Fifteen

Two weeks later, Private Detective Jason Ripley checked his watch. Exactly ten o'clock on the dot. He pressed the bell with his pudgy finger, then once more wiped the moist palms of his hands on his coat. In the twenty years that he had been in detective work, he always found that the most uncomfortable moment came just before you rang the bell. Instinctively he knew that trouble always answered. This time the trouble was a very attractive woman who had opened the door and stood smiling at him nervously. "Are you Mrs. Humphrey?" he asked in a quiet, confidential tone.

"Yes," she replied. She glanced from left to right as if she were checking to make certain that no one saw him enter. "Come in."

"My name is Ripley," he said pleasantly as he stepped inside. "Going to be a nice day out." As he entered the living room he sensed how tense Mrs. Humphrey was, and how apprehensive she seemed about the situation.

"Would you like some coffee?" she asked immediately.

Coffee would give them both something to fiddle with, he thought. "Yes, indeed I would. Thank you very much. I would indeed like a cup of coffee." When she disappeared into the kitchen, his searching eyes missed nothing. He liked thinking of himself as having practically a scientific, unbiased sort of observing mind which noticed everything, excluding nothing. However, he refrained from arriving at conclusions. His clients usually did that for him. As he cast his eye about the room, he felt that there was something funereal about the atmosphere. There was another presence missing. There was a vacancy, an emptiness in the house. Mr. Humphrey, no doubt. He stood up politely as she returned with a heavy tray.

"Mr. Rogers called yesterday afternoon to say that you would be coming," she said, placing the tray carefully down on the coffee table.

"You did ask for a report every two weeks?" he peered at her mercilessly.

"Oh yes," she acknowledged.

He felt better. For a moment he imagined that there might have been a mistake at the agency. "What we do, Mrs. Humphrey, is very simple. We give you personalized service rather than a written report. Our customers like it better that way. Any data that we might have uncovered during the two weeks that have just passed we naturally bring here to you. In case the information should be urgent, we let you know immediately by phone."

Mona watched him carefully. "Then you've discovered nothing urgent?" she asked hopefully.

But Detective Ripley wiggled his lips thoughtfully. "Not exactly that. What I would say is that what we have discovered is not damaging. Mr. Humphrey leads a rather, shall we say, routine existence."

Thank God, thought Mona gratefully. Then there isn't any woman involved. "Do you take sugar or cream?" she asked him.

"Just black will do it," he replied. Cautiously he reached inside his coat pocket and took out a small black notebook, fingering its smudged pages reverently.

"Your coffee?" She handed him the cup.

After sitting the cup down he shoved his pudgy fingers against each page slowly, shoving back the paper one page at a time until he found what he was looking for.

"Detective Ripley," she asked hesitantly. "There's no possible way that my husband might ever suspect...."

Detective Ripley's face became terrifyingly red. Did she have any idea of what she had just asked him? "Mrs. Humphrey," he began indignantly, "A bricklayer lays bricks. A truck driver drives trucks," he swallowed agonizingly, "and a detective detects. *He* is not detected."

"Sorry," she apologized. She had no idea that a detective could be so sensitive about his profession. She nodded in the direction of the little black book that he held crushed to his chest. "Would you tell me what it is you have...." she smiled, "...detected?"

"Indeed I shall," he replied, holding the note book up close to his eyes. He began reading in a monotonous but efficient manner. "Your husband leaves here in the morning at eight o'clock sharp. If it is not raining, he walks to work. If it is, he rides on the bus. He takes the same route however when he is walking. He usually arrives at his office around eight twenty-eight. He has his lunch punctually at one."

My God, thought Mona irritably. Am I paying him to tell me what I already know myself?

But Detective Ripley was not to be deterred. On and on he went with this and that until he was all but out of breath. However," he said in an ominous tone, for this was the moment he had been waiting for, the moment when the client suddenly changed places with him. That superior calmness would drop now right before his eyes, then he would feel superior. All the time he was hiding behind parked cars and in doorways his client was relaxing at home, waiting for the results, but now his turn had come. "However," he said again with emphasis, relishing the way he had caught her undivided attention. Her pretty face became strained with alertness. The eyes softened with fear and suspicion. Her chin trembled with infinite possibilities of deception. "He has been seeing a great deal of young lady. Especially over the weekends." That did it. Her calm mask dropped completely.

"A young woman?" she cried out.

He could see right inside that mind of hers, all the wheels buzzing around and round, checking off each possible suspect. Was it Mary? No. Maybe Irene? No. Oh, the whole spectacle was too funny for words. All the menial spying made up for by this irreproachable, delectable moment. He had been compensated now. For another two weeks anyway.

"Twice they had lunch together at the *Carriage House*," he went on ruthlessly. "In fact, the very next day after you sought our help we followed them there. Or rather she met him there. He was late."

"But what does she look like?"

He smiled sympathetically because he could see she had not stumbled across a possible suspect. "She's about nineteen or twenty I would say. Very well dressed. Her grandmother lives here in Georgetown. Apparently she lives with her although we have not been able to verify that fact as yet."

"What's her name?"

"Anna Martin," he replied gently. He was thrilled even more this time because he could see that the name meant nothing to her. A real deception. And Mr. Humphrey had seemed so mundane, so uncomplicated and consequently boring.

Mona repeated the name over and over as if she were tasting an unpleasant flavor. "But I don't know any Anna Martin," she exclaimed angrily, practically suggesting that he must be mistaken.

But he went on stoically. He had been accused of lying before. "Her grandmother is Mrs. Leighton Ross." He waited to see if that meant anything. "Her husband died about five years ago. The home is over on P Street." He took out a little white card. "Here is the address."

She stared at the card in her fingers for about a minute, stood up abruptly, then flung it resentfully down on the table. "I don't believe it. I just don't believe it."

Detective Ripley took up his cup of coffee now. This was his moment to relax. His intermission. He had started the ball of suspicion rolling, so there was nothing else for him to do now except drink his coffee and wait. She would walk back and forth across the living room, having it out with herself. This was a very crucial moment. She could become angry with the information, blame him and fire him on the spot. He had to be careful how he handled her from now on. If she became greedy, however, for more facts, then he realized he was safe.

Detective Ripley had come to think of this particular moment as his cozy little "Moment of Truth," that he had read so much about in bull fights and psychiatric books. In fact, there were moments like this when he felt exactly like a psychiatrist who had just confronted his patient with a most unpleasant fact. The truth. And you never could tell exactly how a human being would react to that. There had been cases when he had seen broken, suspicious clients suddenly rise up, supported by a dazzling amount of strength once the facts were brought out in the open. Other times, he was regretful to say, he had seen handsome, self-assured men and women collapse both physically and mentally right before his very eyes. Even though he felt sorry for most of them, he did have his job to do, and he would do it to the bitter end. The truth is what they had hired him to find out and that's exactly what he gave them. He was not responsible for the results.

Now, he was not exactly certain of Mrs. Humphrey. She had class behind her. Years of composure and certainty. Her emotions must be tucked away like woolen socks in a cedar chest. She was a much more complicated woman. Real strong defenses. Detective Ripley tried his very best to remain emotionally out of the situations he found himself investigating. The few times he had seen Mr. Humphrey and young woman together he had felt, however, a certain harmless sympathy for the both of them. The young woman he could see was most certainly in love with him but he seemed never to enjoy their, he learned this word from a spy story, tête-à-têtes. There was still something about their relationship which puzzled him. They did not *look* like lovers. There was not that sinful guilt lingering nearby. They were too out in the open about their behavior. They never peered behind each other's shoulders to see if they were being followed or recognized by friends.

"Detective Ripley," she broke rudely into his intermission. Her face was composed and there was a defiant glint in her eyes. "Have you anything more you wish to tell me?"

He checked his notebook. "Last Sunday afternoon they were down at Fisherman's Wharf. They went into one of those seafood bars and had shrimp." This time she looked stricken.

Michael had told her he was going down to the office to work on the Gorgon case. "Anything more?" she flung at him.

"He sent her a bottle of Arpège from Nordstrom's," he announced proudly, for he had been very clever about discovering this fact. Instead of going himself for the gift, Mr. Humphrey had sent one of the government drivers instead. Detective Ripley had a hunch after seeing them talking together, so he had followed and later checked with the salesgirl.

"Is she very pretty?"

"Well, Mrs. Humphrey.... he said, standing up because he always found this kind of question embarrassing. "Beauty is a very personal matter, isn't it? It's in the eye of the beholder. The woman I might think is pretty you might not think is. Understand what I mean? But I will tell you this. She strikes me as being a very nice young woman. Not flashy or loud. Well brought up. Just a nice girl."

Now Mona knew she was in danger. "And there's nothing

else then?" she questioned him carefully. After all, he could be hiding something.

"Not a thing," he said with a smile. He knew exactly what she had been fishing for. They had not been in bed together.

"Well then," she said, moving towards him. "I'm sorry to have to rush you off like this, but I've got an appointment this morning."

"I quite understand," he said with a knowing twinkle in his eye. Her appointment was with the nearest telephone.

"Thank you for coming, Detective Ripley." She opened the door hastily.

"In two weeks' time then?" he said, stepping out on the pavement and disappearing like a shadow.

She slammed the door shut angrily, and running back into the living room, she flung herself down on the couch, wanting more than anything else to be able to cry, but no tears came. Instead she beat furiously with her fists into the first pillow she got her hands on, then flung it with great force into the corner. "Damn him. Damn him," she cried out. He *was* going to destroy everything. And that nice girl was going to help him. They were plotting, those two, to ruin her marriage, and she was helpless to prevent it. Her eyes fell on the card. She stared at it as if the card might bite. She thought a moment, then impulsively she jumped up and ran towards the telephone. She dialed the number. While the phone buzzed she went over hurriedly in her mind a possible plan.

"Hello, Bea? Yes. Yes. Are you going to be busy for lunch? Would you like to come over here? Over there? Will you be alone? Yes. That's right. I want to see you alone. Fine. Around twelve-thirty. Good. I'll see you then."

After she hung up, she sat there pensively, her eyes getting larger and larger with determination. She went back over to the table and picked up the card. She hurried over to the telephone book, checking the address against the names in the book. Yes, there it was. Her first impulse was to call Mrs. Leighton Ross right away, but then, wouldn't a surprise attack be better? After all, didn't she want to see this nice girl face to face? She laughed out loud. "I can't wait to see her expression." She glanced down at the card again. "Miss Anna Martin, you're about to meet Mrs. Michael Humphrey." Then she stood up, and for the first time in her life she wanted a drink at ten-thirty in the morning.

Chapter Sixteen

Mrs. Ross sat in her upstairs sitting room alone. She was just about to begin a letter to her daughter, only she was disturbed because she could not decide on exactly what type of letter she wanted to write. She had picked up her pen several times, hesitated, then placed it back down on the desk. Her thoughts were disturbed because what she wanted to discuss with her daughter might very well seem to Anna, if she should find out, to be a slight sort of betrayal. However, this time, Mrs. Ross after picking up the pen, touched it gently to her lips, then began writing:

My dearest Martha,

I received your engrossing letter in the mail this morning. I could tell instantly that you have become exceedingly worried over Anna, and that you are quite anxious for her to be coming home soon. You know, of course, without my saying it that I have been more than delighted to have her here with me like this, and if she did leave, a great deal of pleasure would depart with her, but this time, I will not plead with you to let her remain a little longer. In fact, this time I would urge you to get her home with you as soon as possible.

I have not mentioned what I am about to write you before, mostly because I felt it was not, in the end, my business. Anna has not confided in me too much about the matter nor has she exactly hidden it from me. You see, Martha dear, Anna arrived here in a very disturbed state of mind. She felt all sorts of little silly guilts about having left the convent, fearing most of all, I should say, disapproval. Of course, my not being a Catholic helped the situation a great deal. But the poor child was desolate; so in need of someone to take her out of herself. Even I could not help her too far there. Apparently there is always a limit to what we can do for people we love, isn't there? Especially for the people we love.

Now, on the day that she arrived here, she met a gentleman, I hesitate to say where because you will certainly accuse me of not looking after her properly, on one of her walks to Dumbarton Oaks. The first time that she mentioned him, I really did not pay too much attention to what she said. She spoke of him fleetingly. However, a few days later after the meeting she apparently saw him again. You must understand that this was not by any prearranged plan, just merely a coincidence. I'm certain of this point, Martha. Anna may omit information but she would never falsify it. Now I did not know of this meeting until a day or two after it had occurred. I was aware that she was dazzlingly happy all of a sudden. I hesitate to say even this to you, dear Martha, but I felt, she never said, that she was beginning to act very much like a young girl in love.

As the days passed here, she told me more about this gentleman, a Michael Humphrey, and how he had asked her to have lunch with him on Saturday. I, of course, would not hear of it. But she begged and pleaded so beautifully, and seemed to be in such a wretched state that in the end I relented. Now, at this point, something even more puzzling came into the picture. Instead of coming here to the house to pick her up and to meet me, of course, he called, it seemed to me at the very last *minute, to ask if she would mind very much meeting him directly at the restaurant. He was at work, he said, and could not make it on time. I will not say that I was suspicious then. After all, such things do happen in the business world. But since then they have been seeing a great deal of each other, and up to this moment, he has never once set foot in this house.*

Yesterday I decided that things had gone far enough. I waited until she came in from her walk. I questioned her, telling her that such questioning was necessary from my point of view because I could not let the situation continue without feeling responsible for any danger that she might find herself in. She told me right then and there, which was a complete surprise, that she was just on the verge of asking if Mr. Humphrey could come for tea tomorrow, which is today. She said he wanted very much to meet me. Well, Martha, dear, what was I to say to that? She had knocked the branch from right under my feet. There was no point in pursuing the questioning I had decided on since he would be here himself to answer them.

However, instead of walking away with a certain dreamy look in her eyes, a look which has become a personal part of her behavior, she sat down beside me and began to confide, it's the only word I know for telling such strange facts, that poor Mr. Humphrey was in a greatly disturbed state of mind due, as I understood her to say, to the fact that he had been involved in an accident lately where the car in front of theirs hit and killed a small boy instantly. A most regrettable happening surely. But it seems that Mr. Humphrey has not exactly been able to put the scene out of his mind. The little boy's death preys, as she said with pity in her voice, on his mind. I will say that all of this part needs clarifying but I am certain we can wait on it. I would not like to put such personal questions to him on our very first meeting. Perhaps he will volunteer the information on his own. There are more important questions that I would rather bring up.

Next, I took the bull by the horns, as I do quite frequently now since your father died, a role I am becoming more familiar with being an old woman alone in the world and on her own, and asked Anna outright if she was in love with him. She blushed in that charming way of hers. Surely that was her answer, Martha! Is he in love with you? I asked next. From this question I got quite an entirely different reaction. I could tell immediately from the manner in which she hesitated that she could not honestly reply to that question because she did not know the right reply. "So," I said, "then it is just as well he is coming here. I can see for myself."

Anna is now out in the garden this very moment planting, you won't believe it, some June lily bulbs which I was able, after all these years, to purchase from Mrs. Mansfield. You know how she put me off from the very beginning. Anna loves doing it. The convent at least channeled her energies or taught her how to. So when your letter came this morning I thought it best to write you the truth. (I have not mentioned to her the content of your letter, however.) I assume that you have suspected something from Anna's letters. You don't mention any facts, more an uneasy feeling, so I presume that she has told you as little as she has told me. However, with Mr. Humphrey coming like he is for tea in just a few hours, I will be able to tell you much more tomorrow morning.

Martha, I am certain that I have heard his name before but I can't think where. He will no doubt clear that up too. Please let me hear from you soon, Martha *dear, and I will do whatever you and Henry advise. I promise to keep writing you developments as they occur. In the meantime, know that your mother thinks of you frequently, especially since she has your dear daughter with her as a reminder.*

My fondest regards to you both,
Mother

Chapter Seventeen

Michael had told no one, not even Anna, where he was going. He had made the appointment for the morning so that he would be able to tell Anna exactly what had happened and what he hoped to do with his life when he saw her in the afternoon. He couldn't wait to see the expression on her face when he told her.

The monastery was some distance outside of Washington, sitting up on top of a steep hill. Michael had never been inside one, and as the taxi sped up the twisting road, he felt trepidations, because what he was about to do was so completely against everything he believed in. Once the taxi reached the top they found themselves in front of a two-storied stone building. On the left side was the chapel. Michael paid the driver, watched the taxi leave, then turned around, faced the front door, only he hesitated. Was this the destination he had been heading for since he was born? The monastic life? Was that why he had never been comfortable with the life he had been living in the world? He rang the bell.

While he waited, he was aware of birds twittering in the pines, pines that grew plentifully about the buildings. Deep within he was even more aware of a peaceful feeling, which, like a wild bird newly domesticated, had calmly settled down inside his being. For once he felt he was making the best decision for himself. It had been the right decision for him from the very beginning, only he had not realized it, had not understood his needs. If only his grandmother could see him now. He smiled to himself as he thought of Lourdes. Suddenly the door opened. "Good morning," he said self-consciously, "I have an appointment with Father Gregory."

The monk bowed him into a small sitting room. "Wait in here. I will call Father Gregory. He told me he was expecting you, Mr. Humphrey." He closed the door silently behind him as he left.

Michael sat down on one of the huge overstuffed chairs. He noticed the furniture. Some chairs were carved grotesquely with no cushions. Only wooden seats. Others were skinny but substantial-looking with velveteen cushions. He realized that the odd assortment must have been donations from friends. But even so, stability was there in the room with him. There was no getting away from it. Anna had been right. Permanence was deep within the walls, even in the bleeding Christ that hung precariously from a heavy substantial walnut cross. In here was a sample of life everlasting. In here was peace. In here, then, was God. He heard the sound of footsteps approaching outside, and when the door opened, a tall, heavyset monk appeared with a welcoming smile on his lips.

"I am Father Gregory," he said, in a deep, deep voice, his brown eyes were gentle but shrewd. They took in Michael's appearance instantaneously, noticing the texture of the clothes he was wearing, the tone of his personality, the intensity of expression on his face, the lack of sleep in his eyes, the shape of his discontented mouth. "What can I do for you, Mr. Humphrey?" He remembered the urgency in the man's voice on the phone. He knew his situation was desperate.

Michael noticed that the monk sat down on the most uncomfortable chair in the room, the skinny one with no cushion. He felt guilty for being comfortable. Then he felt guilty for feeling guilty. "Father," he began, "I've never had much to do with the clergy before. I am not remotely aware of how to begin."

"There is no beginning, Mr. Humphrey," said the monk devoutly. "There is only the now. What I suggest is that you tell me what is important to you, what prompted you to pick up the telephone to call me. That is where the beginning is in this instance."

"What prompted me?" he echoed. How would it sound if he put it into words? If he spoke his feelings aloud? "Father, I can't run away from myself anymore. I've come as far as I can alone. I need God. I need his help." There. The truth was out. Like a tooth. Extracted painlessly. He no longer had to pretend to himself.

"Aren't you a Catholic?" asked Father Gregory carefully.

Michael shook his head.

"But why do you come to us?" The monk sat up straight now. He was interested.

"I met a Catholic girl not so long ago who had been in a convent. She had left because she decided that she did not have the proper vocation for a nun."

"But what has she to do with you?" asked the monk.

How could he ever explain her influence. "Father," he began, his face was full of earnestness, of a deep desire to be honest. "For the last two years I've known that something was wrong with the life I was living. I'm married and have two children. But it's never been enough. Lately I've become more and more aware of my inner poverty. A few weeks ago I was at the end of my rope. I didn't know where to turn. What to do. Then one day I met this girl, Anna, just by accident. (Or was it just by accident?) She had just gotten out of the convent that day. Gradually, as we began to know each other better, what she was telling me about the religious life seemed to be exactly what I was hunting for. She had not been successful as a nun and I had not been successful as a father and as a business man. Bit by bit I began to see why I had failed."

"But failure is not a good reason for wanting to…. What is

it you want to become, Mr. Humphrey? A Catholic or a monk?"

Michael protested. "Don't you see what I mean, Father Gregory? Before, I didn't know if there was a God or not. Before, I didn't know nor did I even care. But now, now I find that it doesn't matter to me one way or another. About the proof, I mean. If there isn't one, I've got to create my own. I can't live without God any longer. I can't give my life any purpose without Him. That's what I've come to. I know it now."

"Ah!" said Father Gregory in a reverent whisper. "That's quite a different matter." He smiled patiently over at Michael. "That is not failure then," he said proudly. "That is success. The Hound of Heaven has tracked you down at last."

"The Hound of Heaven?" Michael repeated bewilderedly.

In his lifetime, Father Gregory had interviewed hundreds of human beings who wanted to enter a monastery. There seemed to be just as many reasons for wanting to enter one as there were for any other profession. Many novices were neurotics who wanted to run away from life, so they ran right into the monastery for shelter. Usually, they did not last very long. Then there were those poor souls who needed to suffer. They turned the simplicity of life within the monastery into deprivation, and the austere routine into punishment. The mind usually rebelled sooner or later, exposing their masochistic inclinations. So the greatest problem of all was to learn how to winnow out the false vocation from the true, if possible, right from the start. Each year they took in so many novices and gave them a trial period. If they survived the first year they went on into the second and third before they were actually received into the order itself. There was something just a little bit different about Mr. Humphrey which caught his curiosity. He was not in the least saying what the others usually said. Or rather, he was saying exactly what the other novices would not have said in the very beginning. They would have been more cautious. Less direct. Usually the majority of candidates were exceedingly emotional about their vocation. The fervor smoldered out of their eyes, in the way they genuflected and passionately touched the water in the fonts.

But there was no such fervor coming from this man. He seemed to have arrived at his position very logically, very realistically and above all, rationally, which, as Father Gregory knew by now, made for the most comfortable vocations. "What exactly is it you want from us?" Father Gregory asked.

Michael glanced over at him with solemn eyes. "I would like to be able to stay here for a few weeks. I would like to be able to talk with someone about religion, about this order. But more than anything else right now, I want to be by myself so that I can think, so that I can try and understand what has been happening to me. At home I can't do it. My wife knows that something is wrong. She makes me feel uncomfortable and I feel guilty because I can't tell her why. But how can you explain this kind of thing to your wife, who you know won't approve?"

"In other words," said the monk simply, "You are asking us for sanctuary?"

Michael felt embarrassed by the word. Could you ever find a sanctuary? Weren't there sanctuaries and sanctuaries? Couldn't you make the world a sanctuary from yourself? In this case he guessed he was asking for sanctuary, only he hoped a sanctuary *to* himself. "Yes," he said hesitantly. "I guess I am."

The monk smiled understandingly over at him. "Notice, Mr. Humphrey, I said sanctuary, not an escape. Don't mix them up, will you? I suppose through the centuries we have given sanctuary to every kind of person you can imagine, from kings on down to rascals of every sort. I don't see any reason why we should make an exception here in your case. That's what we're here for. Of course you may come and stay as long as you like."

Michael blushed with gratitude. "I thought," he stammered

nervously, "That I would tell my wife this evening and if it's all right with you, I would return tomorrow with my bag."

"We can make arrangements for that," said the monk. "But what will your wife say?"

"I don't know," he admitted. "I haven't told her anything about this yet. I wanted to wait until I was sure that I could come here. I'll tell her this evening."

"You realize, of course, that even if you should decide to become a Catholic and want to join our order that we would not be able to condone your leaving a wife and children in order to enter the religious life unless she were agreeable. She would have to agree not to marry again and you would agree to go on supporting them unless she wishes to make other financial arrangements."

He seemed startled. "I hadn't even thought that far," he replied seriously. "But right now I think the most important thing for me to do is get settled here and see what develops before I make any definite decisions."

"You're very right," said Father Gregory. He stood up. "Would you like me to show you the rest of the monastery?" After all, he thought, there really is no point in getting too seriously involved in personal discussion until he has lived with us long enough to make up his mind what he wants. Perhaps a week here would end his quandary. In a week's time he might very well want to return to his wife and children.

As they walked along the hallways, they passed other monks, usually in pairs, who seemed to be hurrying for an immediate destination. "We teach," volunteered Father Gregory. "That is our primary secular function. We have a school adjoining the monastery. We try to keep one foot in this world and one in the next. I don't know if you know much about the history of our order...."

"Yes," said Michael proudly, "Anna told me a great deal."

"Did she tell you about our community life?"

"No," he said shyly. "I just thought that they were all about the same. I mean similar to what the nuns do."

"Not exactly," instructed the monk. "Some orders are contemplative. They pray and fast and often they have taken the vow of silence."

"That must take a great deal of courage and patience," suggested Michael.

Father Gregory laughed. "Sometimes I think not half as much as it takes to live here like we do. Our community varies at times from twenty some to almost thirty. Without the grace from God we would find it most difficult living together like we do. Each one of us is from a very different walk of life. Sometimes I think that the only thing we have in common *is* God."

"Without the grace from God?" queried Michael in a confused tone.

"Of course," explained the monk, stopping outside the chapel door. "Without His grace we would not be able to stand one another for more than a week or two. But with this special grace we are patient with each other." He pulled open the door to the chapel and as he stepped inside, he knelt, dipped his hand into a small white marble font, then stood up again. He held out his still-wet fingers to Michael to touch.

Self-consciously Michael touched them, then made a week sign of the cross. "Father," he said in a low, embarrassed voice, "I've never prayed in my life."

The monk looked surprised. "But you want to learn to, don't you?" he asked with a frown on his face.

"Learn to pray?" Michael repeated in astonishment.

"Yes," he replied gently. "I think one has to overcome a feeling of self-consciousness before one can realize the soothing effects of prayer. And you, Mr. Humphrey, are extremely aware of yourself."

Michael was offended by this remark. Surely it was a

reprimand. Outside in the world (he had already begun to think in terms of inside and outside), most of the energies were spent on making the individual realize his own money-making potentials, in becoming more aware of what he was and who he was. Of being able to assert himself comfortably. Of being able to exploit painlessly as well as to be painlessly exploited. Self-assertion was guaranteed by the Constitution. But here, in the monastery, self-effacement was a virtue, a goal. As Anna had said to him many times, in the religious life it is not *your* will but *His* will that counts. Would he have that much self-denial? Would he have that much patience with himself? Oddly enough, he suspected that the more you gave into His will, the more God asserted His will on you, so consequently it was not self-effacement exactly as much as an assertion towards a larger, more powerful self that was God.

"This, as you can see, is our chapel," explained the monk, his arm outstretched. "We have mass here in the morning, then we meet here before lunch, then before we retire in the evenings."

As they passed through long corridors, the more uncertain Michael became. There was so much that was alien to him, so much that he felt he would have to learn and understand about the Catholic religion. He sensed the thickness of its history, and like the labyrinthine corridors they were passing through, he sensed the mystery, the ritual, the endless walks into eternal comprehension. Whenever he saw monks strolling or gathered together in small groups he was acutely aware of time passed, of another era, medieval mostly, and he felt that these cowled men had gotten lost or had strayed from a 14th century monastery, walking right into the present. They were, in a sense, like the dinosaur, extinct, but it was the doctrine which they adhered to that kept them alive and in the present.

"Here we have the cloisters," said Father Gregory, pointing to a long, long corridor where one after another door opened into small rooms. On each door was painted in black letters a particular saint's name. "Each monk has his own room." He opened the door. Michael glanced in, saw a small bed, a wash bowl, and in the far corner was a kneeling bench. "You can practice how to pray on one of those," joked the monk happily. "Now I'll show you Brother Francis' beehives. Brother Francis tends them with loving care."

Outside the sunlight shimmered brilliantly over everything. As they approached the apiary, Michael could hear the soft hum of the bees as they flew in and out of the thirty hives that sat majestic and yellow on small white platforms. The humming caressed his eardrum pleasantly.

"The warmth from the sun is just beginning to bring them out of hibernation. The bees keep staggering out into the sunlight like they've been drunk all winter long." A thin, middle-aged monk came walking towards them. "This is Brother Francis," introduced the monk. The bee keeper's face was serious but his eyes were gentle and shy. So shy he could hardly glance over at Michael. "They'll be out full force today," prophesized Father Gregory. The brother nodded his head silently in agreement.

As they turned back towards the monastery, Michael couldn't help but ask, "Father, what would you do if you found yourself in my situation?"

The monk stopped short. "Your situation?"

"I mean if you suddenly felt you had to have God in your life?" stammered Michael.

A gleam of humor danced in the monk's eyes. "I'd do my very best to find Him." The monk studied Michael for several minutes. "I know what made you ask that question, Mr. Humphrey. Wanting to go into the monastery and being in one are two entirely different propositions. Perhaps being exposed to us like you just have been makes you feel that the reality of a religious life might be too much for you to take at this point.

When you come here tomorrow, I don't think you should allow yourself to think too deeply on the possibilities of a religious vocation. What I feel is more important for a person like you is to be exposed to a place where God is considered, where His will is our will. In the world you have as many wills as there are people to exert them. Here, we try to have only one. His. I believe that you will either be quite at home here or miserable. However, there is only one way for you to find that out and that's by staying here for a few days. Remember this, Mr. Humphrey, that you are not the first to come here for sanctuary, nor will you be the last."

"But Father," cried Michael in desperation. "I never wanted to come to God out of fear."

"Dear Mr. Humphrey," said the monk sternly, "surely, it would be a fine thing to come to God out of pure love, but isn't it better to come to him through fear than not at all? God is no good to anyone unless there is a human need for Him. Remember that. Each one of us here has come to Him by very different paths. But once we are on that path, our destination is the same. It does not matter *how* we found it, just as long as we *have* found it. And that path teaches us to know and serve His will."

To know and serve God's will. Somehow the very idea of it frightened Michael. As far back as he could remember he had been fighting to extricate himself from the many wills that had surrounded him, that had shaped him into the person he was today. Some had been beneficial, others had not. Once again he recalled the scene in Lourdes, the heads bowed low, the candles held in sweaty, hot hands, the sound of the human voice raised in song, begging, pleading, hoping. A strange sickening taste flooded his mouth. His stomach felt odd. Was this what was meant by bowing to God's will, this abdication of self? Even now he fought against the idea. Surely God was the welding together of oneself with the strength of God. Not the down-on-the-knees, tears-in-the-eyes, words-on-the-mouth kind of religion. Was this what was being demanded of him? he wondered. What he knew he wanted was an affirmation, a deep meaningful cry of joy, of strength inside himself so that he could affirm the magnificence of God in man. The Word made flesh, as Anna had said. It seemed to him that this public display of fervor, this open sickness of religious fever was self-indulgent. To cling to God, to want His meaning to be your meaning was not to pull Him down with you, nor did He wish to pull you up with Him. To Michael his need for God was real, was purposeful but he hoped not too self-indulgent an act. To know and serve God's will. "How does one know God's will?" he asked gently.

"God sent His only begotten Son down to reveal it to us," replied Father Gregory patiently. "And the Catholic Church is founded on those teachings. You have a great deal to learn, Mr. Humphrey, and you have a long, long way to go."

Michael wanted to protest for the monk seemed so assured, so positive. Was this God's Self talking? Or Father Gregory's? Or the Catholic Church? To Michael the long, long way to go was life. The lantern to guide and the stick to aid on that journey was God. Death was the final destination. As long as one was alive one had a long, long way to go. In a way he envied Father Gregory, for he had found the path, and apparently he was in a position to know exactly where he, Michael Humphrey, was on it. Somehow, he had stumbled on that path by accident, with Anna perhaps, but he knew now that he could not turn away. "Yes," he admitted proudly. "I do have a long, long way to go."

Chapter Eighteen

The moment that Mona walked into the living room, Beatrice Drake could tell she had been drinking. She didn't know how she knew but she knew. Mona was very careful not to meet her eyes. Perhaps it was the sudden way she put out her hand as she walked into the living room that gave Beatrice the clue.

"Well," joked Bea, "I see you've been busy this morning."

Mona seated herself carefully on the couch. She tried to smile but the fact that she was still uncertain of exactly how much Bea might know about Anna Martin made her smile look forced and ugly. Then too, she should never have taken that second highball. "I had a visitor," she replied mysteriously, "If that's what you mean."

"A visitor?" said Bea laughingly. "Anyone I know?" she started for the bar.

"You might," replied Mona lighting a cigarette. "His name is Jason Ripley, and it's not the *Believe it or Not* Ripley either."

"What did he want?" Bea reached for the bourbon.

"He was a detective," Mona volunteered casually.

Bea's fingers clutched tightly around the neck of the bottle. "A detective?" repeated Bea. She took the cork out and poured them each two ounces of liquor. Neither one of them spoke. She clonked ice into the glasses, filled them up with water and turned around. "Mona, you didn't hire a detective to follow Michael, did you? " She walked over, handed her a glass, then sat down next to her on the couch.

Mona glanced away from her gaze.

"That's a very foolish and dangerous thing for you to have done," she said quickly. "What do you think would happen if Michael ever found out?"

"What do I care what would happen?" she defended herself. "He doesn't give a damn what he does to me, does he?"

"Listen, Mona," said Bea, sitting her drink down on the table. "Michael is a very fine person. If he hasn't told you what the matter is, then he doesn't know himself. The moment he finds out he'll come tell you."

Mona laughed derisively. "You really believe that, don't you? He's even got you fooled."

"I don't think Michael hopes to fool anyone," Bea said indignantly. "I think he's a very honest human being."

"Oh, you think he's a very honest human being," argued Mona, squinting her eyes because her vision was slightly blurred by the highballs. "Well, I've got a secret to tell you about Michael." She took a long drag on the cigarette she was holding nervously. "Michael's a fraud." She nodded her head at Bea as if to emphasize the truth. "He always had been. You've always thought of him as being the strong, silent type. Well, he isn't. He hasn't got any will power. He's really a very weak person, Bea. Without me, he'd never be where he is today."

"He may not be a very forceful person," admitted Bea. "But that doesn't necessarily mean he's weak."

"He is," she sang out angrily. "He is weak. He couldn't leave me on his own. He had to go out and find somebody else to help him."

"Somebody else?" Bea leaned forward.

"That's right." Mona bit her lip. "He's been running around with her for weeks." She snapped open her purse and took out the card. "Miss Anna Martin," she said flippantly. Then she mimicked the detective. "A very nice girl."

Bea stood up, "I don't believe it," she said hesitantly.

"Michael isn't a deceitful person."

"You don't know what it's been like living with him," Mona cried out protesting. "He's always kept things hidden from me. He always has. I don't know what he thinks I'm going to do to him. After all, I am his wife. I've had his children. Don't I have a right to know what he's thinking?"

Bea retorted, "Listen, Mona, no one has a right to know what anyone's thinking unless they want to extend that right. Maybe that's why he doesn't tell you what he's thinking because he knows you'll try to take him over completely. Did that ever occur to you?"

"Are you insinuating that I'm a domineering wife?" Mona struggled to stand up.

"I think you're even worse than that," said Bea, losing her self-control. "I think you're a damned fool, which in my book is ten times worse."

"So you're going to take his side against mine?" cried Mona, reaching for her purse. "Why is it no one will ever take my side?" Before she could continue, she burst into tears.

"His side?" went on Bea as if she had not noticed that Mona was crying. "Your side? What's this got to do with sides? You keep talking about your marriage as if it were some sort of tennis game you were playing." She watched Mona searching feverishly for a handkerchief. "I just can't believe that you would do a thing like that. Hire a detective to follow Michael. It's indecent. If you can't ask him to his face what you want to know...."

"I did ask him. I swear I did," she sniffled out. "You don't know how many times I asked him what was wrong. Only he would never tell me. And now he's found a very nice girl."

"You mean the detective told you he had found this girl." She emphasized the word *detective*.

"Now don't try to put the blame on Mr. Ripley," said Mona, blowing her nose noisily. "He didn't make her up. She lives right on P Street. With her grandmother. I've checked the name in the telephone book. He's been seeing her every weekend."

Bea watched her carefully for several moments. "Well," she began. "You're going to ignore it, aren't you?"

Mona looked up at her as if she must be mistaken. "Ignore it?" she cried out in disbelief. "How can I ignore infidelity?"

"But you don't know that Michael's been unfaithful to you," insisted Bea. "Did that detective of your say they had?"

"No," admitted Mona, tears began again. "But I just feel that he has been."

Bea shook her head in exasperation. "I never imagined that a woman as sensible as you could behave as idiotically and as adolescent as you are right now."

"Adolescent?" Mona blew her nose again. "Just because I want to defend my marriage?"

Bea shook her head again. "Mona, there you go again. Defend your marriage. It isn't just your marriage. It belongs just as much to Michael as it does to you."

"Then why does he want to destroy it?"

"Did he ever say he did?" asked Bea sharply. "But if you're not careful you're going to destroy it single-handed. He won't have to do one thing. You'll see to that." She sat down on the couch next to Mona and took her hand. "Listen, dear, just ignore the whole thing. When Michael's ready to tell you what he wants to tell you, he will. Have a little faith in him."

"I can't any longer," explained Mona. "How can you have faith in someone when you know how weak and cowardly they are inside."

"Then why did you marry Michael?" asked Bea, staring her straight in the eye.

Mona looked away guiltily, "I thought he needed my strength."

"I see," Bea began to laugh.

"Why are you laughing at me like that?"

"I'm not laughing at you exactly, dear," said Bea standing up. "I'm just laughing at how ridiculous human beings can behave at times. Let me fix you another drink."

"I don't think I'd better have another one," Mona said cautiously. "I've got to keep a clear head."

"A clear head for what?" repeated Bea.

Mona realized she had said too much.

"A clear head for what?" repeated Bea.

Mona looked down at the purse in her lap.

"Mona," said Bea softly. "You're not thinking of going over to see that girl?"

Mona glanced defiantly up at her. "That's exactly what I'm going to do as soon as I leave here."

"I don't believe you," Bea said aloud. "You wouldn't be that foolish."

"I'm not foolish," defended Mona. "I'm that honest."

Bea came back at her immediately. "Mona, we've known each other for a long time now, haven't we? You can trust me. I think you know that. Well, dear, believe me, this isn't the way to handle a situation like that."

"It's the way I'm going to handle it," she said, adamant on the subject.

Bea studied her face carefully. Yes, she thought, that's the way you really are going to handle it. And the worst part is you're going to feel so righteous about what you are going to do. That's the saddest part.

Mona remained silent.

"I suppose it won't do any good for me to try and talk you out of it, would it? I can see how determined you are just by the way you sit there." A pause. "He'll never forgive you, Mona. You know that. Even if he has been unfaithful to you. It will be the end of everything between you two." Another pause. "Even if Michael is, as you say, weak, he must still have some pride left. Weak people seem to need more pride than strong ones sometimes." A longer pause. "Mona, think it over first. Take your time. Don't plunge into it carelessly. There's one thing you can't ever put back together again and that's a human relationship. They never mend. The glue won't harden. The pieces don't fit properly again. There's always a difference."

"I've made up my mind, Bea," said Mona sternly. "There's nothing you can say to change it."

For a moment, Bea thought of calling Michael. But then, wouldn't she, too, be taking sides. "You know, Mona," went on Bea, hoping for the last time to talk her out of it. "I told you I had been married twice before I married the Senator. I learned a lot from those experiences. I even had to go out to Reno. I watched the other women, listened to what they had to say. Most of them wandered around like they were lost. The ones that could afford it gambled or drank from sunup to sundown. But the one thing that impressed me most about those women was the fact that when a woman gets indignant, feels that her pride has been tampered with, she can do an awful lot of foolish, wasteful things in return. Out in Reno they had time to reconsider, to look back on what they had done. I don't think too many of them were particularly proud of their behavior. Most of them had taken their fear of being alone, of being rejected, and made it into all sorts of decent causes, like honesty and understanding. They would have given anything to have had a second chance. Some of them, even though they were out there getting a divorce, still refused to let go inside. I suppose it's a form of punishment. Sometimes a woman thinks that if she can make her husband suffer like she has, she'll get back something in return. Look at life, realistically for a change. Do you think that even if you went over to see this girl, you would be able to destroy their relationship without damaging your own with Michael beyond repair?"

"Please," cried out Mona angrily. "I don't want to hear any more of your wonderful wisdom. It's very easy for you to sit there and say be patient, be understanding. You aren't involved. But my whole life is at stake. My children. My happiness. Do you think I can just sit next door and do nothing about it? Do you honestly think that, Bea? You must know me better than that. Maybe they can do that sort of thing over in Europe but I can't. All I want to know is the truth. What has been going on between Michael and this girl? If I don't like what I discover, then I'll take the necessary steps to protect myself. But I refuse to sit over there day in and day out driving myself crazy wondering what he is doing, where he's gone. It just wouldn't be fair," she cried out bitterly. "It just wouldn't be fair."

Well, I've done all I can, thought Bea. She'll just have to learn like the rest of us. "How about having a little lunch now?" she suggested.

Mona dried her eyes. She nodded her head. She even tried to smile.

Chapter Nineteen

When the doorbell rang, Mrs. Ross was out in the pantry arranging a bowl of flowers. She checked the time on her jeweled wrist watch. "That couldn't be Mr. Humphrey," she called to Mary, who was in the kitchen. "Why, it's just three o'clock." She listened to the soft sound of Mary's footsteps as she padded towards the front door. Next she heard a muffled conversation going on in the hallway. Then Mary's footsteps padded back again. "Who is it, Mary?" she asked without looking up from what she was doing. She poked another jonquil into the center of the bowl. When Mary did not reply, she glanced up. "Well...?" she saw confusion expressed on the maid's face. "Who is it?" she asked hesitantly.

"She said," began Mary reticently, "that her name was Mrs. Michael Humphrey."

Mrs. Ross' hand stopped in midair. The fern that her fingers held fell from her hand onto the table. "Mrs. Michael Humphrey?" she whispered. She understood at once what the name meant. "Please tell her that I shall be right in." As the maid started out of the pantry, she called, "Is Miss Anna in her room?"

"Yes, Ma'am," replied Mary.

Mrs. Ross nodded her thanks. After Mary had gone back into the hall, Mrs. Ross stood there, uncertain of exactly what she would do next. Call Anna? No, better to find out what she should do next. "Mrs. Michael Humphrey?" she said aloud, trying hard to believe the name was real. She picked up the fern she had dropped, then carefully inserted it in between the jonquils. "There," she said proudly, picking up the arrangement and heading for the front of the house.

As she entered the front parlor, she watched an attractive, dark-haired woman stand up. "I'm Mrs. Ross," she said pleasantly, placing the bowl on one of the tables.

"And I'm Mrs. Humphrey," she said with emphasis on Mrs.

"What can I do for you?" asked Mrs. Ross, moving towards the woman.

Mona hesitated. "Mrs. Ross," she began with a certain amount of reticence in her voice. "Do you have a Miss Anna Martin living with you?"

Mrs. Ross nodded her head. "She's my granddaughter."

"Then I think it would be best for me to speak with her," said Mona. There was no point in secondhand interviews.

"Do you mind," said Mrs. Ross, making a gesture with her hand for her to be seated, "telling me why?"

"I'd rather not," came the reply.

Mrs. Ross stood there debating. "Mrs. Humphrey," she said diplomatically. "I suppose there is no reason for us to fence with one another. Even though I do not know your husband, I am aware that my granddaughter is acquainted with him." She smiled very cordially. "In fact, he is to be here this afternoon for tea."

"For tea?" Mona echoed her surprise. She had never seen him drink a cup of tea in her life.

"Of course if I had known that he was married I would have insisted that you come too."

"Then your granddaughter is not aware that Michael is married? That he has two children?" From the shocked expression on the woman's face she knew that neither one of them knew.

"From what Anna has told me, Mrs. Humphrey," went on Mrs. Ross, trying her best to sound casual, "I would say that she is not aware of these facts."

"I'm here to make her aware of these facts," said Mona forcefully.

"I see," Mrs. Ross also saw a great deal more. This woman was in no mood to be trifled with. She saw that no matter how calmly she sat there, inside she was having a great deal of trouble controlling her emotions. Mrs. Ross even suspected that she might have been drinking. "I think," she began quietly, "that it would be easier for me to make her aware of those facts than it would be coming from you, Mrs. Humphrey."

"I don't intend to make it easier for either one of them, Mrs. Ross," snapped Mona irritably.

Mrs. Ross looked straight into Mona's eyes. "Are you inferring that your husband and my granddaughter...."

"I'm not inferring anything, Mrs. Ross," retorted Mona angrily. "I'm here to find out."

Mrs. Ross felt suddenly that under no circumstances should this woman and Anna meet. At all cost she must keep them away from each other. There was no telling what harm she might do to Anna. She was dangerous. She was ruthless. And above all, Mrs. Ross knew that she was mistaken. She sat down across from Mona. "Mrs. Humphrey," she smiled understandingly. "I am afraid that it will be impossible for you to see my granddaughter. She is staying with me and is under my care. I cannot allow you to disturb her needlessly. I will be perfectly willing to speak to her about...."

"Needlessly?" cried out Mona furiously. "Needlessly? Listen, Mrs. Ross, I'm not leaving here until I see that girl."

"I think that you are being exceedingly rude, Mrs. Humphrey," said Mrs. Ross, standing up.

"I may very well be," admitted Mona. "But I'm not leaving here until I see here." She stood up also. "Do you think for one moment that I enjoy having to come here like this, to humiliate myself? Do you think that I like having to question a woman about her relationship with my husband?"

"Then why are you doing it?" intercepted Mrs. Ross.

"Because I want a little peace of mind, that's why. If my husband is having an affair with your granddaughter—"

"Really, Mrs. Humphrey!" cried out Mrs. Ross. "I must insist that you leave here immediately. I think you must be overwrought and don't quite know what you are saying. My granddaughter and your husband are just friends, Mrs. Humphrey, and nothing more."

"Then why are you so afraid to let me see her?" asked Mona, feeling that she had won a point. "What harm would there be in having her meet Michael's wife?"

At first Mrs. Ross did not reply. She could only stand there motionless. What harm would there be? Why was she behaving so protectively towards Anna? Yet, she realized instinctively that there would be a great deal of harm. "Mrs. Humphrey," she said, sitting down across from her. "Let me appeal to your understanding. My granddaughter is only twenty years of age. She spent the last year in a convent. She had hoped to become a nun eventually, only the life didn't seem to suit her. She was under a great deal of strain. A few weeks ago she came here to visit with me. She was in a very unhappy, anxious state. You see, she felt that she had failed everyone she loved in some way. She had no one to turn to. She was lost and needed someone badly. Now, I've never met your husband, but he seemed to be able to give her back her belief in herself." She faltered. "I know that she is very devoted to your husband. She told me that. I do not know, however, what his feelings are about her. That's why I would rather tell her myself. I wouldn't want to have to destroy the little self-confidence she had acquired in these last few weeks needlessly."

Mona laughed rudely. "Needlessly?" she cried out. "Mrs. Ross, you don't seem to understand. Those two have been seeing each other continually. Every weekend they've been out somewhere together while I sit home with the children. Do you call that needlessly?"

"But I promise you," said Mrs. Ross, "I promise you that once she understands that he is married she will of her own accord end the relationship. Anna is a very fine young woman."

"I'm sure she is, Mrs. Ross," said Mona impatiently. "But I'm not going to take the chance."

Suddenly Mrs. Ross realized why she insisted upon seeing Ana face to face. "What you really mean, Mrs. Humphrey," said Mrs. Ross curtly, showing for the first time her own irritation, "is that you want to see her in order to see what your husband might find of interest in her?"

Mona blushed slightly. "Do you blame me?"

Mrs. Ross realized how futile it was to go on. She had met this type of woman before. There was nothing altruistic in her character. She was selfish to the core. Blindly selfish. She thought of Anna upstairs getting herself ready. She could not stand the idea of having her meet this kind of woman. She actually felt sorry for Mr. Humphrey. Why hadn't he told Anna? Could it just be possible that he had, only Anna had not told her? No, Anna would never do that. Maybe that was why he was coming to tea. To tell them both. "Then there is nothing I can say to change your mind?" asked Mrs. Ross quietly.

Mona shook her head. "Not a thing."

"Very well." Mrs. Ross stood up. "I shall call Anna." Slowly she walked out of the room with her head bowed. She walked into the kitchen. "Mary, will you ask Miss Anna to come down, please? There is someone who wishes to see her."

As Mrs. Ross stepped back into the hallway, she paused, leaned against the wall for support, then shook her head. Poor Anna! That lovely world she had been living in these past weeks was going to crash down about her without any warning whatsoever. And I am helpless to prevent it. I don't even want to think of the possible consequences. When she stepped back into the parlor, Mrs. Humphrey was lighting a cigarette. "I've sent for her," she said in a tired voice. "I hope, Mrs. Humphrey, that you will get a great deal of satisfaction out of what you are about to do."

Mona glanced at her through cold, angry eyes. "I expect to, Mrs. Ross. You can believe me, I expect to." She mashed out her cigarette vindictively.

Mrs. Ross hesitated by the door. As she heard Anna's footsteps coming down the stairway, she stiffened. Would she ever forgive me? wondered her grandmother. Would she always associate me with this scene?

"Where are you?" called Anna.

"We're in here, dear," replied Mrs. Ross, stepping out into the hallway, wishing there were some way she could prepare her granddaughter.

"We?" said Anna, her face brightened up. "Has Michael come already?"

Mrs. Ross shook her head. Tears sprung up in her eyes. "Oh Anna!" She wanted to explain but she could not go on.

Then Anna glanced into the parlor and saw the woman sitting there. She turned back to her grandmother for an explanation but all her grandmother could do was reach out and squeeze Anna's arm either in affection or in order to encourage her. "Who is she?" asked Anna softly. Her grandmother only shook her head. "Nothing's happened to Michael, has it?" she asked the woman, walking towards her.

A bitter smile formed on Mona's lips. She got up from the sofa and walked towards Anna. "No, nothing has happened to Michael, Miss Martin. And nothing is going to either."

"But I don't understand," said Anna, looking back at her grandmother for an explanation.

"Then let me help you to," said Mona, stopping in front of her. "I'm Michael's wife."

The flush of her cheeks vanished like crusts of snow melting under the hot sun. Her ears heard but didn't hear. Her eyes looked but didn't see. "Michael's wife?" she whispered.

"Yes, Miss Martin," smiled Mona. "His wife."

Was that cry echoing through her brain ever going to end? Would her legs hold her up even though she knew all her strength had disappeared. "But he never told me...." she explained.

"Apparently not," remarked Mona. And she meant it. The color on Miss Martin's face was ashen. Mona expected her to faint any moment. She didn't miss the victorious gleam in the grandmother's eyes either. "I'm sorry that I had to come like this, Miss Martin," she said hesitantly, "but I'm afraid that it was the only way."

"His wife?" Anna repeated again. She still could not believe it nor accept it.

"And he has two children too," said Mona relentlessly. This shocked Anna even more. She seemed stunned by this revelation. Her expression of disbelief gave way to actual fear. Mona went on. "For the past two weeks I've had you followed by a detective, Miss Martin. I know that you and Michael have been seeing a great deal of each other. Under the circumstances, I must ask you not to see him again. Obviously he hasn't been honest enough to tell you that he was married. He forces me to take that responsibility."

"But I just can't believe it," cried Anna. Why hadn't he ever told her? Would it have made any difference in her feelings for him? Somehow or other, even though she felt the temptation to condemn him, there was something missing which made such a judgment impossible.

Mona began to put on her gloves. "Well, Miss Martin, that's the kind of a person Michael is. He's never really been honest with anyone."

"Please," interceded Mrs. Ross. "Haven't you done enough?"

Mona stared resentfully at Mrs. Ross, then turned her attention back to Anna. "Miss Martin, it's very apparent to me that you have grown very fond of Michael. I think your grandmother underestimated the extent of your feelings. However, I am sure she would agree with me that it would be best if you stopped seeing him. I know that you would not like being named as a correspondent in a divorce case." She passed Anna and stopped before Mrs. Ross. "Thank you for letting me see your granddaughter. I don't think it takes too much imagination to see how things were going with them. Certainly my coming here was the most sensible way."

"Do you?" Mrs. Ross did not wait for a reply. She walked out in the hallway and opened the door. She wanted her out of the house as quickly as possible.

Mona understood.

Once the door was closed, Mrs. Ross hurried back into the parlor. Anna had not moved from the center of the room. She stood rigid like a statue. Her hands were clenched by her side.

"Anna," cried Mrs. Ross helplessly. "That was a dreadful thing for that woman to do. So heartless. So inconsiderate."

"I think the truth is always heartless," replied Anna tensely. "I think that she was right. Coming here was the only sensible way."

"Oh Anna!" sobbed Mrs. Ross, touching her shoulder sympathetically. "I had no idea how much you had come to care for him."

Anna shook her head in puzzlement. "But why didn't he ever tell me? That's what I don't understand. Why he never told me?"

"Poor man!" said Mrs. Ross gently. "Maybe he was afraid to."

Anna glanced pathetically into her grandmother's eyes. "Is it always going to be like this, Grandmother? Is life always going to be like this? So much pain. So much hurt. So much failure. Is it? Is it?" She broke down and began crying. She flung herself onto one of the sofas.

"There, there, dear," said Mrs. Ross comfortingly. "That's better." She sat down beside her, patted her back. "Cry out your pain. That's the best way. Cry it out." She rocked her gently from side to side as she had rocked her own children many years before. "That's what tears are for. To ease pain. It's like a thundercloud. When it can't hold any more, it rains."

Anna lifted her tear-streaked face. "I don't think that I want to live if life is always going to be like this. I can't bear it, Grandmother. I just can't."

"My dear," instructed her grandmother, "I'd hate to count the times I have felt that way, but thank God, the feeling is only transitory. We forget pain easily. We want to. We only want to acknowledge the good things, the bright things, the easy things. It's only through pain that we expand, broaden our perspective on life. You can be certain that where there is no pain there is very little vitality. So dear, just cry it out. That's right. It helps so."

* * *

When Mona returned home she poured herself out a stiff shot of whiskey. She was trembling. For the first time in her life she had gone out and met the enemy face to face. But oh, that face, she thought sadly, that shocked, pale face. But after all, wasn't that shocked, pale face the face that her husband had been gazing into each weekend? Little sensitive girls shouldn't play around with other people's husbands. Only Michael had lied to her. No, he never lied. He simply avoided the subject that he was married. She took another shot. God, she thought regretfully, I wish I could see Michael's face when he goes there for tea. She laughed out loud thinking of it. It would be worth everything just to see his expression.

Chapter Twenty

Michael stopped to buy a dozen yellow roses for Mrs. Ross. As he stood in the shop nervously watching the florist sorting out the prettier buds (he was nervous because he was late), his thoughts went back to the morning he had spent in his office after returning from the monastery. He had felt so relieved, so secure from anxiety about what he had done, that he found himself plunging into work, plunging into the Gargon case with a zeal he had not felt since his first days out of law school. In the midst of his feverish anxieties he tried to examine his feelings, his sudden spontaneous desire to work, to improve, to achieve. At least I'm feeling something now, he admitted proudly.

But underneath his self-investigation he was aware that some sort of climax, some sort of danger had been met and apparently overcome that day on the Memorial Bridge. The experience of witnessing the actuality of death, of its suddenness, of its unfairness, of the objective brutality of death, of staring at suffering face to face, of seeing the patient acceptance of fate on the mother's face, had acted traumatically on his personality. He had felt as if the monotonous world he had been existing in had been ripped apart, exposing him, finally, to reality. He could almost swear that he had heard a rushing of wind about his ears as the air swirled in to fill up the vacuum that had been himself. In some way that he did not understand, that dreadful, searing, futile expression on the mother's face had gouged into his most inner self, forcing it up like some hibernating animal into daylight. Like the beginning trickles of snow melting in the early spring, his feelings had begun seeping into his consciousness. As each day passed, the little trickle had become a small stream, and once more he was conscious of being alive, of time passing, of being part of life, of living, only, he had to have a support to sustain him, a hand to clasp, something to believe in. Man, he had decided, was too unreliable. God was the only support he trusted now.

And Anna, of course. How patient she had been. How understanding! Answering all of his persistent questions, never reticent with her answers. Always direct. Always honest. Always interested. Actually, he had to admit this too, but wasn't it her sense of piety that had infected him in the beginning? Hadn't he envied her inner strength, her desire to want to believe in something, of having reached out for God's Hand, regardless of consequences?

As he watched the florist wrapping up the roses, he realized how much Anna had changed from the person he had met in Dumbarton Oaks that day. She had been exhausted, and worn out emotionally but as the days passed, each time he saw her she had become more alive, more sparkling, more happy.

He recalled a very important conversation they had had one Sunday down at Fisherman's Wharf.

"Anna," she had stopped her as they were walking along by the boats. "How did you imagine that you had been called by God? I mean, how did you feel?"

She smiled, "Why do you keep asking so many questions about the religious life?" She looked into his eyes. "Sometimes I even think that you want to enter a monastery yourself."

Had she guessed? he wondered.

"But how did you *feel*?" he insisted.

She tried not to think back that far, back to those days when her Paradise was shimmering there on the horizon, bright and clean with promise. "How did it feel?" she echoed. Could she tell him she felt like she was feverish for something deep and satisfying? Could she tell him that at night when she was in her bed, surrounded by darkness, she was overcome by such a penetrating, sinking feeling of being alone that she had to compensate for it by offering herself up to Christ in order to blot out her sense of helplessness as a human being? "Maybe that's the feeling," she said aloud. "Maybe we just have to get rid of a deep inner feeling of helplessness. We want relief. Some people find it in their work. Others keep busy all the time. Some people are lucky to find it in each other. They fall in love. But then there are those whose loneliness can't be ended so easily. Only God can relieve that ache, that void."

That ache! That void! He paid for the roses and walked out on the street. Hadn't she, after all, put her finger on his whole problem? That ache? That void? He walked along briskly. He was attempting now to fill it up to the brim with God. Certainly it was his only answer. But first he needed, what had Father Gregory called it, sanctuary. There was something so unreal about what he was doing yet real enough that he felt he could reach out, reach out and touch the walls, both visible and invisible, that the monastery offered. For the first time in his life he realized that he had a purpose, a goal of his own. And that goal was to learn who God was, to discover inside himself what God wanted of him and what he wanted of God, and certainly in that investigation he would come to love Him. Again, what was it Father Gregory had said? To know and serve God's will. Such a tremendous undertaking.

As he turned up P Street, his thoughts drifted to Mona. Would she ever understand what he felt? Would she ever let him go? He was afraid to consider her position. He knew that she was not a woman who let go easily. After all, if he had filled that ache, that void for her, he could understand why she would not want him to leave. And the children? What about them? Long ago he admitted to himself that they meant very little to him. They had had them, he suspected, because Mona wanted to complete the picture of a happy, modern marriage.

Perhaps in the beginning it would be best not to mention the idea that he was thinking of entering a monastery. Just tell her he was going away for a while. Maybe that would be easier. But would it be fair? Wasn't he postponing the inevitable? After all, hadn't she the right to know what the possibilities of the future were? Yet, suppose he told her, then in the end, like Anna, failed. What if that ache, that void could not be filled by God? What then? Would he be able to return to Mona? Would she take him back?

He stopped in front of the large yellow house on P Street, smiled happily at the thought of Anna waiting inside, and how much he had to tell her, then youthfully he hurried up the steps and rang the bell. Then the door opened and he gave his name to the maid. He was sensitive enough to notice a certain disturbance in her expression. "Mrs. Ross is expecting me," he asserted. "I'm to have tea." He smiled nervously.

She nodded her head. "Wait in there, sir," she said, pointing to the parlor.

She's not too friendly, he thought as he entered the room. He quickly noticed everything in the parlor, remembering that this was the safe past that Anna enjoyed so much. All of it there, in the cameo broaches, in the rings worn and memoried, in the feathered fans, in the lockets, in the exact way certain photographs were placed on the tables. He heard someone coming. Turning, he was surprised to see Mrs. Ross standing in the doorway alone. She hesitated before she spoke "Mr. Humphrey…?" she began.

But he interrupted her. "Mrs. Ross," he said as charmingly as he could. "I'm afraid I'm a little late."

Mrs. Ross intercepted. "Mr. Humphrey, what are you doing here?" She seemed angry.

"Doing?" he replied dubiously. "Why, I'm here for tea?

Didn't Anna tell you?"

Mrs. Ross entered. "Mr. Humphrey...." She seemed weary suddenly. "Apparently you don't know?"

"Know what?" he asked in alarm. "Nothing's happened to Anna?"

"A great deal has happened to Anna." She could tell by his expression that he knew nothing of what had occurred earlier in the afternoon. Even though she tried to be polite and solicitous she knew that her behavior was forced and she deplored false behavior in anyone. "Mr. Humphrey," she began, holding up her hand for him to be silent. "Why didn't you tell Anna you were a married man?"

For a moment he seemed stunned. He stared at Mrs. Ross as if he were trying to figure out why she had asked such a question. "I didn't tell her," he said honestly, "because I didn't think it made much difference."

"Much difference to whom?" Mrs. Ross asked antagonistically.

"What I meant was, Mrs. Ross," he explained, "That my being married had nothing to do with our relationship."

"Apparently you are not aware of it, Mr. Humphrey," said Mrs. Ross, moving towards the settee, "but your wife came here this afternoon to see Anna."

"My wife?" he exclaimed.

"Yes," smiled Mrs. Ross, bitterly remembering. "She came because she felt that she was entitled to interfere with a relationship that she was felt was detrimental to her."

"But I can't believe it," he said, completely baffled. What had made her do such a thing?

"Your wife, Mr. Humphrey, hired a detective to follow you." She watched him flush angrily. "In following you, poor Anna was uncovered. Your wife came here to, well, the only word I can use effectively would be the word *threaten*, but politely, you understand, Mr. Humphrey. She threatened Anna not to see you again unless she wished to be named as a correspondent in a divorce suit."

"But I can't believe that Mona would ever do a thing like that," he said unbelievingly. "Mona could never do a thing like that."

"You can believe me, Mr. Humphrey, that your wife not only did do it but, in my opinion, is capable of much more in protecting her own happiness when she feels it is being threatened."

He bowed his head. "I'm very sorry that she behaved like that. It must have been most annoying."

"Annoying?" exclaimed Mrs. Ross. "You don't seem to understand the full implication of her visit, Mr. Humphrey." She studied his face carefully. "No, you don't, do you?" She could see it all plainly.

"Understand?" he asked bewilderedly.

"Mr. Humphrey," said Mrs. Ross, holding on to the edge of the settee. "Did it ever occur to you that Anna might have fallen in love with you?"

"Fallen in love?" he cried out.

"I see," said Mrs. Ross quietly. She did see. His innocence was scattered across the features of his face. That he could have been so unaware of Anna's feelings aggravated her, but as she watched the painful awareness creep across the innocence, she actually pitied him. He paled noticeably and for a moment Mrs. Ross was afraid that he was going to faint. "Sit there," she directed, pointing to a nearby chair. He still had the yellow roses in his hand. As he slumped into the chair, they fell from his grasp to the floor. Really, thought Mrs. Ross, he is too pathetic. "Mr. Humphrey," she called gently.

But he spoke out of a daze. "I thought we were friends. All this time we...."

"Mr. Humphrey, don't blame yourself," she said softly. "After all, you are not responsible for Anna's feelings."

"The idea never occurred to me," he went on. "She seemed so happy, so alive...." There was no need for him to go on. There was the key. So happy. So alive. Now he understood. Her laughter, her smile, her lightness, her flushed cheeks and sparkling eyes. "Where is she now?" he asked, turning towards Mrs. Ross with tears in his eyes.

"She's in her room," said Mrs. Ross. "She doesn't want to see you. She asked me to come down to see you instead."

"Doesn't want to see me?" he repeated incredulously.

"Don't you understand, Mr. Humphrey?" Mrs. Ross checked a sympathetic urge to reach across and touch his arm. "What your wife did this afternoon left her with very little. I'm afraid she devastated Anna with her frankness."

"My wife?" he said, as if he were beginning to come out of his daze. "You don't mean that she knew about Anna's feelings? You don't mean that she came here and deliberately and...."

"I'm not certain that she knew before she came," affirmed Mrs. Ross. "But she had only to look at Anna to know once she was here."

He stood up agitatedly. "And then deliberately threatened her?"

"Exactly," said Mrs. Ross, feeling the humiliation of the scene all over again.

For the first time in years he felt anger rising within. He had faced many sides of Mona's personality but he had never imagined she was capable of cruelty, deliberate cruelty. And what a ridiculous position she had put him in. But he supposed that was part of the satisfaction she was seeking. "Did Anna say anything?"

"What was there to say?" replied Mrs. Ross agitatedly. "You had told her nothing about your wife and two children. Your wife had her in every direction. Anna was helpless in the face of facts and in her own feelings for you."

"I still can't believe that Mona would ever do a thing like that."

"Well," said Mrs. Ross patiently, "There is Anna upstairs crying her eyes out."

Silence. They could hear cars out in the street. Life was going on busily around them but there, in that room, it had stopped for the moment.

Finally, "Mrs. Ross," he asked, What can I do?"

"There is nothing to be done," she said wisely. "Everything has already been done."

"But I can't leave here letting Anna think that I had deliberately deceived her," he insisted.

"Are you certain that you didn't, Mr. Humphrey?" asked Mrs. Ross. She stood up suddenly.

"No," he protested furiously. "I could never deceive Anna."

"Perhaps not deliberately. Perhaps not consciously...." continued Mrs. Ross, but she stopped abruptly. In the mirror she saw Anna's reflection watching them both from the doorway. "Why, Anna...." she called out, turning quickly to face her. Michael turned around. "What are you doing down here?" admonished Mrs. Ross, crossing solicitously towards the door.

Anna hesitated shyly. In her hand was a crumpled handkerchief. She wanted very badly to look at Michael but she was afraid of behaving foolishly.

"Really, dear, you should have stayed in your room," said her grandmother, looking with uncertainty from Anna to Michael as if she were making up her mind whether she should leave the two of them alone together. "Mr. Humphrey was just about to leave," she suggested.

Anna looked at him directly now with stricken eyes. "Why?" she whispered with difficulty, her eyes filling up again with hot feverish tears.

"You must not let yourself become upset again," warned

Mrs. Ross. She glanced pleadingly at Mr. Humphrey for help. "Really, I do think you should leave."

But Michael ignored her efforts. Instead, he turned his attention to Anna. "I didn't understand," he explained self-consciously. He asked Mrs. Ross, "Won't you let us alone for a few minutes? I can't leave like this. Anna, it isn't fair. You have to let me explain."

Anna glanced hesitantly from his face to her grandmother's. "I'll be all right," she said finally, in a choked voice.

"Mr. Humphrey, you've caused enough trouble," persisted Mrs. Ross. "I don't want her disturbed like this. Perhaps another time might be best."

"Look," he said impatiently, "if I leave now you'd probably never let me in here again." He appealed directly to Anna. "Please let me explain, then you'll understand. Please."

Anna nodded her head, smiled at her grandmother, then walked over towards the mantel. "I'll be all right, Grandmother. Please leave us alone."

Her grandmother made no effort to reply. She simply looked with disapproval from one to the other, then left.

Anna saw the roses lying on the floor. She bent down to pick them up.

Michael was embarrassed. "I brought them for your grandmother," he explained.

Anna tried to smile appreciatively. "She likes yellow roses very much."

Michael stopped still in the middle of the room. "Anna, I didn't know my wife was coming over here today," he cried out defensively. "I don't understand why she behaved like that."

"Do you think the *why* is important?" asked Anna, laying the roses down on the table.

"Yes, I do," he replied emphatically.

Anna watched him for a second. "The *why* is because she is in love with you."

Michael's gaze faltered guiltily.

"Does that mean that you are not in love with her?" Anna dared ask.

"Anna," he said, moving towards her. "Please let's sit down. I've got something very important that I want to tell you."

She hesitated, then quietly she walked over and sat down on one of the settees. He sat down across from her. He looks like a little boy about to make a confession, she thought.

"I don't know exactly where to begin," he stammered. "I mean, I don't know exactly where it *does* begin. So much has happened to me so suddenly." His expression became intent and there were traces of a blush on his cheeks.

Oh no, thought Anna frantically. He couldn't be going to tell me that he is in love with me.

"Do you remember the first time that we met each other in Dumbarton Oaks?" She nodded her head. How would she ever be able to forget it? "Do you remember that you noticed right away how unhappy I was? Then we began talking about you. You said that you had just come out of a convent. Do you remember? And I kept refusing to believe you?"

"Yes," she assured him. "I remember that part very well." She had often wondered what he meant.

"Well," he said painfully. "The fact is that I've never believed in anything or anyone in my life. I've never had any interest in too much of life. Some people seem to care about everything. Houses. Furniture. Cars. But for me there's never been anything."

"Not even your wife?" Anna asked in astonishment.

"I tried with Mona," he explained reluctantly. "The only problem was that her interest lay elsewhere. Or maybe I should say her interest lay everywhere. Mona is perfectly adjusted to her times. I'm not. I got lost years ago."

"Got lost?" echoed Anna questioningly.

He nodded his head. "I guess if you don't keep up with the

times you fall behind. Well, I'm way behind. All the values that I believe in seem to have become obsolete overnight. I just lost my way. Then on the day that we met, I knew it for a fact. You made me realize it. I did need help and I needed it badly. But where do you turn for it? Nowadays, I guess the usual place is the psychiatrist. He tries to pull you back into the stream of things, into the present. You get to flowing with the crowd again. With me the trouble seems to be deeper than that." He smiled ironically. "With me, Anna, there was that ache, that void you talked about. With me it was all or nothing. I suppose I wanted someone or something to believe in with everything that was in me. That kind of belief would be my only salvation. That's all I've been hunting for since I've been alive. I've yearned for a cause that was great enough for me to give myself up to completely."

"And have you found it?" she asked, holding her breath.

"Yes," he said shyly. "I think I have."

"What is it?"

He smiled patiently. "No, it's who is it?"

"Who?" Anna was unable to sit still another moment. She stood up abruptly, walking towards the mirror. She did not turn around but watched him through the glass. She was trembling visibly. She knew that she was not the type of person that another could make a cause of. She could not accept that much love, or that much responsibility. She was not that strong. She would split apart at the seams. All she could ever hope to contain was herself. He had no right to place her in such an awkward position. No right at all. And wasn't he forcing her to face the fact that she was not, in the end, capable of receiving love? Yes, she could certainly offer it to another, but how much more it took to receive it. "Tell me quickly," she begged suddenly. Her eyes never left his face. "Who?"

"God," he said simply.

"God?" repeated Anna in a hushed voice. She turned around

to face him directly. "God?" she repeated again. She was suddenly caught between the desire to laugh at her own vanity or cry at having been so mistaken about herself. But that one word rang like a clear bell. That one tone seemed to clear up the confusion immediately. God? It had been Him all along. From that first moment in Dumbarton Oaks. She had mistaken his interest, believing that it was she he was interested in. She couldn't quite believe it. All this time her rival had been God and she had never even suspected. All those times they had been together, they were only opportunities for him to ask her questions about her vocation, her beliefs. Somewhere in between the desire to laugh and the desire to cry was her love for him. She stared at him, wanting more than anything to be angry, to hate him, to accuse him of leading her on, but in reality, she knew that he had done nothing. She had simply led herself on.

"Aren't you going to say anything?" he asked, a hurt expression appeared on his face.

"What is there for me to say?" she asked cautiously.

"But don't you see," he went on, trying to make her understand. "You helped me. You showed me the way."

"No," she cried out angrily. She didn't want to hear it. She had brought on disaster to her love. All these weeks she had thought she was constructing a firm foundation for it, only now, he was sitting there telling her that she had, in fact, removed with one hand what she had been constructing with the other. "I don't want to hear any more." She put her hands to her ears.

"But I haven't told you the rest," he insisted.

"Could there be any more?"

"This morning I went up to that monastery that you told me about. They are going to let me stay there with them for a few days until I can get myself straightened out. I've got to understand what's been happening to me."

"Yes, of course you do." And I, she thought, have got to

understand what's happening to me.

"Anna," he said hesitatingly. "Your grandmother told me you had come to care a great deal for me. I'm very proud that you have."

Come to care a great deal about him! How understandingly he had put it. If he only knew. First she had lost Christ and now she was losing him. Twice now she had put all of herself into someone else and twice now she had failed. The strain was really too great. Too great and too deep. And he was hunting for a cause to put himself into completely. But wasn't everyone? Weren't the causes disappearing one by one? In the end, wasn't she the only cause that she could put her energies into? Wasn't that what was happening all over the world? The Paradises were shrinking one by one. The horizons were getting smaller. God help him, she thought. He'll need it. "Michael," she said softly. "I understand. I really do. I mean about what you want and what you've been searching for. Don't worry about me."

"Anna," he said intently, but with dignity. "Forgive me.... Forgive me for not understanding, for not thinking more about you than myself.... Forgive me...." The moment he said, "forgive," the word seemed to echo and vibrate deep within his memory until once again he saw the expression on the stricken mother's face, saw her muted pain, and heard the driver's 'forgive me's' tinkle like pins dropped into an empty glass. Why do we have to go on hurting one another? he wondered. Why keep inflicting pain? And once we wound, that plea for forgiveness comes welling up into the mouth. That's too easy. "To ask forgiveness is too easy," he said aloud to Anna. He hated himself suddenly. "No," he said unexpectedly, standing up. "I don't want you to forgive me. I don't want anyone to forgive me. I don't want to forgive anyone. That's too easy. We should have to bear our mistakes. We shouldn't pawn them off on Christ, or on each other. I don't want God to forgive me.

Forgive us our trespasses as we forgive those who trespass. No, forgiveness cancels out everything. We won't learn. We won't have to bear out our mistakes."

Anna was shocked. He seemed to be behaving peculiarly. "Michael," she said tensely. "I think you had better go now."

"You'll let me come back, won't you?" he asked.

"We'll see," she said, hurrying towards the doorway. He followed her submissively. At the door, even though she tried not to look into his eyes, she realized that in all probability this would be the last time they would see each other. "Good-bye," she said faintly.

Unexpectedly, he reached out for her hand, held it up to his lips, then kissed it. Then he touched the palm to his cheek reverently. "Pray for me," he said timidly, then turned and walked out of the house.

Anna closed the door quickly, then leaned against it as if she were shutting out a flood that was pounding outside. She strained against it as if she were afraid the water might force its way in and engulf her. "Please," she cried out inside herself. "Please, someone help me." She looked heavenward. Only there was no answer. Tears scalded her cheeks and her thin body trembled with sobs.

Later, when Mrs. Ross found her, she was sitting curled up on one of the settees. The shadows had deepened in the corners. "Anna," she called warmly. "Shall I turn on a light?" Anna did not answer. She continued to sit there staring in the corner. Mrs. Ross clicked on the light. "Dinner will be ready soon. Mary's baked a nice custard." She moved in front of her granddaughter, then decided that it was safe to sit down next to her. "Ah," she exclaimed suddenly. "Where did those yellow roses come from?" She reached over to pick them up from the table. "They're wilting."

Anna stared at the roses for a second then glanced up at her grandmother. "He brought them for you," she said softly.

"Oh?" remarked Mrs. Ross. Full of embarrassment she remembered. "How kind."

When Mary came in to announce dinner, she found them both sitting there silent and still. Mrs. Ross had placed the roses back on the table.

Chapter Twenty-One

"Now go to sleep immediately," Mona called irritably up to her children. She sat down by herself in the living room. Next to the chair a light burned provocatively alone in the darkness. He had never come home for dinner. He had not even phoned her. She sat there waiting for the twist of the doorknob. Once in desperation she thought of calling Mrs. Ross to see if he had been there. In the end, she had made a quick, desperate call to Beatrice Drake but because she still sensed that Bea did not approve of her afternoon actions, she had gotten little consolation from talking with her. Then the children had come in. She hurriedly gave them their supper, and hurriedly got them off to bed. Whatever was to come, she did not want them to witness it.

She lit a hundreth cigarette, then for the two hundredth time she glanced expectantly towards the front door, then nervously back to the unopened book in her lap.

Impatiently she flipped the cover and tried forcing herself to read, but the printed lines had an absurd way of moving up and down on the page like a garter snake crossing a dusty road. What are words anyway? she kept asking herself. Who made them? Where did so many come from? She glanced about the half-lighted room, watching the loneliness, like shadows, creeping nearer and nearer. So much she did not understand seemed to be moving in on her. Her whole afternoon seemed crazy and meaningless, yet she had gone through it with deliberateness, with vindictiveness. In fact, hadn't she taken her resentment out on that girl, the resentment she had felt against Michael for deceiving her? Was that fair? Anna Martin's eyes, stricken and confused, looked at her out of the shadows. She could hear the grandmother's haughty words echoing in her ears. Really, the whole day had been a fiasco. Then on top of it all, Michael had not come home. Was he drinking? Was he angry with her? "God, I can't stand this waiting much longer," she cried out angrily, banging her fist down on the arm of the chair.

But at that moment, the door opened and Michael walked in. For a second or two they stared expectantly at each other. She could hardly see his face but she felt his menacing presence there on the foyer.

"Where are the children?" he asked softly.

"I put them to bed," she replied, shutting the book abruptly, as if she were aggravated because he had just interrupted her in the midst of an exciting passage. She made a motion as if she were going to get up but he stopped her.

"I think we had better have a talk," he said tonelessly, as if to say, you'd better stay exactly where you are.

She looked up at him nervously. "I'd better go check on the children first," she said, hoping to postpone the inevitable.

"Look," he said threateningly, walking towards her and into the circumference of yellow light that lay scattered in an uneven circle about the chair. "You've been begging for this talk for the last six months. Now we're going to have it."

She sank diffidently back into the chair. She wasn't going to let him intimidate her. After all, she had discovered enough about him in one day to last her the rest of her life. "Aren't you a little late in getting around to it?"

He did not reply. Instead, he sat down pensively across from her on the couch. His eyes watched her carefully as if he were dreading exactly what approach would be best. He was unusually agitated. Mona could tell just from the uncomfortable way he sat that he was fighting desperately to keep rigid control over his feelings. "Why did you do a thing like that?" he asked finally in a hoarse whisper.

"Do what thing?" she replied, blinking innocently back at him.

"Let's not play games with each other, Mona," he said in a tired manner. All the strength he had seemed to have gone out of him.

Mona was relieved to see that he was tired, even exhausted. That big, righteous scene she had been anticipating with a certain amount of curiosity and fear was not going to come off apparently. He must have got hold of himself before he came in. "You mean," she said flippantly, "let's not play games now that I've found out what kind of games you've been playing."

He knew that she was going to take this attitude. He had been walking around Georgetown trying to figure out what she had been up to, how she would proceed. Finally he had settled on the most unimaginative approach. He had never actually studied Mona's feminine behavior before, consciously anyway, but when he began to take a good look at the past he began to wonder if he had ever understood her, ever actually seen her as she was in reality. Hadn't he, in the end, been living with his own projection of what he thought Mona was about? Hadn't he imagined that she had been living under his standards of behavior? "Mona," he began wearily. "There's no need for us to fight over this. I know you must be quite angry and suspicious of me. I think when I left Mrs. Ross this afternoon I came as near as I ever will in wanting to kill another human being but I've gotten over that feeling now. I've tried to understand. I believe you did it out of panic and personal concern. I don't blame you. If I had the capacity for forgiving you, I would."

"Forgive me?" she cried out furiously. "Forgiving me?" She jumped up from the chair in a second. "What the hell do you mean by that, forgiving me?"

"You should never have gone there to see Anna Martin," he said emphatically. "If you had something to say, you should have said it to me."

"I had something to say to you," she flung back at him, "but you never had time to listen. You just let me sit here with the children while you busied yourself with that girl. I know all about it."

"Yes," he said cynically. "I understand you've had a detective following me."

Mona blushed. "I have to protect myself."

"From me?" he smiled sadly.

"From her," she shouted back. "If you want to have an affair–"

"Mona, you're making a fool of yourself," he cut in. What disturbed him most of all was the fact that after living with Mona for fifteen years they had no real communication with each other. Deeper communication. The communication that cannot be spoken, felt or seen. They had missed that completely. They communicated all on the surface. "I'm sorry that I've done this to you," he said sincerely. "I mean that I put you in such a position where you should become suspicious like this."

"Suspicious?" she flung back at him. "I'm not suspicious any longer. That's what I hired that detective for. Now I know. I suppose you're going to sit there and tell me that you aren't in love with her."

He looked her straight in the eye. "That's exactly what I was going to tell you."

Angry tears filled here eyes. "Don't then," she said. "At least you've never lied to me before. Don't start now. I know all about what you two have been doing. Meeting each other. Buying presents for her. All of it's your fault. I feel sorry for that girl. Never telling her anything. Leading her on."

"You know that isn't true," he said patiently. "We've only known each other for a few weeks and...." He hesitated.

"And?" she forced him to continue.

"And *our* trouble has been in existence from the beginning."

"But you're using her as away out," she accused him.

"As a way out?" He considered the possibility. "I'll admit, Mona, that a few weeks ago I was hunting for a way out because there was a great deal I did not understand about myself."

"And now?" she said, facing him.

"And now I don't need a way out," he said thoughtfully. "What I need now is a way *in*."

"I don't understand what you mean," she said, watching him closer. There did seem to be something different, something restful, or was it a certain contentment or purposefulness about his behavior. He was calm and considerate. More than he had been in months.

"If I hadn't met Anna Martin," he said, trying hard to make her realize how important that meeting was to him, "I might well have tried to find a way out. You see, Mona, Anna had just come from a convent. She thought she wanted to be a nun. Only she didn't have the proper vocation."

"I know," said Mona, sitting down. "Her grandmother told me."

"I met her the very day she left the convent," he said. "I was taking Annette for a walk in the Dumbarton Oaks. The moment I began talking with her I realized that there was something different about her personality."

My God, thought Mona furiously. He *is* in love with her and he doesn't even know it.

"I wanted to know so much about her life in the convent," he went on. "She had so much that she could tell me. But more than anything else, Anna had believed enough in something to dedicate herself to it. To give up the world. I think it was her belief more than anything else that impressed me about Anna." He glanced across at his wife. "Mona, more than anything else, I've wanted something to believe in. I was dying slowly because I had nothing to believe in, nothing to hope for."

"I don't want to hear it," exclaimed Mona, pushing herself back in the chair as if she were breaking the conversation. She hated personal confessions, especially when she knew that what he was saying was true. Why couldn't he have believed in me, she wondered?

"But I've got to tell you," he said urgently. "You've got every right to know."

"Let's not beat around the bush then," she said accusingly. "You're in love. I can tell by the way you talk that you're in love. I can tell by the way you put things, by the tone of your voice, that you want to leave me. That's what all of this discussion comes down to, doesn't it? You do want to leave me?"

"I only want to leave you if you will let me go," he said gently.

"Well," she cried out angrily, leaning across the arm of the chair. "You listen to me, Michael Humphrey. I'll never let you go, do you hear me? I don't care what that girl has done for you. If you think that I am going to be noble, that I'd sit here with two children just so you can go off to her–"

"I'm not going to her," he said quietly.

She stopped. "Where is it you want to go then?"

How was he going to explain it? "Mona," he began cautiously, "if you'd just let me explain what I want to say without interrupting me. What I want to do has nothing at all to do with Anna Martin."

She was completely perplexed. "Who does it have to with?" she asked quickly.

"With God," he said with embarrassment.

"With God?" she repeated, dumbfounded. "I'm afraid I

don't understand."

He took a deep breath. "Mona," he said meekly, "I want to enter the religious life. I think I want to become a monk."

Her first impulse was to laugh. He must be kidding. A monk? As long as she had known him he had never set foot inside a church. While a certain part of her thought of all sorts of clever remarks to make, his eyes forbade her to. There was a new expression on his face, a new certainty in his eyes that she had never seen before. His eyes that looked away from life seemed to be looking right at it now. Right at her. Seeing her. Not around her. "Michael," she said finally, "I'm afraid I don't understand."

"I don't understand a great deal of it myself," he admitted. "But I went out to a monastery this morning just outside of Washington. They are going to let me come and stay with them for a few days until I can decide exactly what it is I want to do. I was coming home this evening to tell you, only I stopped off at Mrs. Ross' for tea and found that you had been there before me."

He had been to a monastery that morning? Why, he actually meant what he was saying. He had made arrangements to stay for a few days. Why, he must be exhausted. He must be overworked. But no, he looks so serious. What he really needs is a vacation. She should have realized. He needed rest and care. She would have to get him away somewhere as soon as possible.

"Poor darling," she said.

"That's one of the reasons I went to Mrs. Ross' today, I wanted to tell Anna."

"You told Anna?" she said. "What did she say?"

"She seemed shocked," he said.

"I should think so," she said. I can't let him go to a monastery like this. Why, suppose someone should hear about it? One of our friends. Or even Bea for that matter. Well, Bea might understand. When she thought of the Senator, she could imagine how he would react. But worst of all, suppose the government ever found out. Why, he would be laughed right out of the organization. They would say he must be having a breakdown of some sort. She need not tell the children. That she could cope with.

"Mona," he said, breaking into her thoughts. "I have to take this chance. I have to go. I've got to find out."

"Michael," she said urgently. "Did it ever occur to you that even *God* might be a *way out*?"

He seemed frightened suddenly. "Then that's what I've got to find out, isn't it?"

"But you can't mean that you would actually leave here and go stay in a monastery?" she cried out.

"I'm going in the morning."

"Michael," she said calmly. "You don't seem to be seeing this in the proper light. What would our friends say if they ever found out? Why, you might even lose your job if any of the men down there should hear of this."

"I can't help what they think, Mona," he said impatiently. Hadn't he gone over all these arguments himself? "I can't go on living like this. I've got to have God. I'm all hollow inside, Mona. Nothing seems important to me. I've got to have someone to believe in. I've got to."

"But what about us?" cried Mona angrily. "What do we do? What do we *believe* in?"

"They wouldn't take me," he said falteringly. "Unless you would agree. It would have to be by mutual consent."

Well, I'll never give that consent, she thought resentfully. If that's what he needs from me, he'll never get it. She started to tell him, but instead she kept quiet. Another thought had entered her consciousness. Was there any great need for her to become so upset? After all, didn't she know him well enough to realize that he would never be able to remain in a monastery for any great length of time? He certainly didn't have what it takes to become a religious. No strength, or did it take strength? Yes, the monastic life must take a tremendous amount of character to survive it, and that, she was positive, Michael did not have. Perhaps the best course would be to let him go. Tell no one. Just say he went away on a business trip. No one would ever need know. Then after a week or two, she would have him back. She would find something for him to believe in her.

However, when she studied him sitting there, there was something disturbing about his presence, something she could not exactly put her finger on. He seemed in some way removed from her reach. Reserved. Set off. What was it exactly? Something about the relaxed way he sat there, the slow easy way he turned his head, the way his eyes looked truthfully into hers. Why, he reminded her of a weary traveler who had been on a long, long journey but had finally reached his destination, only for the moment, he had to rest before stepping foot inside. "Michael," she called out fearfully. She wanted to say, you really wouldn't leave me, would you? But instead she said affably. "Would you like me to fix you a drink?"

He smiled at her maneuver then shook his head. "No, thanks," he stood up. "I'd better go pack."

Pack? The word shook Mona to her firmest foundations. "Of course, dear," she said understandingly. As he walked by her chair she felt an impulse to reach out, to pull him down beside her, but she refrained. For the moment all intimacy must be ended. Any act of closeness would be an intimidation. Later, there would be time for that. She must move carefully now or she might ruin everything. She sat there listening to his footsteps as he walked up the stairs. She heard him overhead. Back and forth. Packing. Packing. The whole situation was absurd. This really can't be happening to me. Who ever heard of a man with two children just casually going off to a monastery? She supposed it had been done but what was even more difficult for her to understand was the fact that after living with him all those years she had never once had an inkling that his problems stemmed from religious origins. Of course, giving a hurried glance over the past few years of their relationship, she realized that he had become more discontent, more dissatisfied with his life, and consequently with their marriage, but would all of his discontentment end with this sudden realization that he needed God? Lots of people feel that they need God, but they didn't have to go into a monastery to prove it.

When he came down finally, Mona was still sitting in the same chair. One more light had been turned on. She had even gotten herself a drink to steady her nerves. She was grateful for one thing. By telling her how he felt and what he intended to do, a great deal of the subterfuge which had existed between them disappeared, enabling them to see each other more realistically, with greater tolerance. With this tolerance came a certain friendliness towards each other, which he mistook for understanding while she mistook it for love, the love that he actually felt towards her but could not express.

Again he sat down across from her with such a patient look about his eyes that Mona became disturbed. Every instinctive nerve in her body was fighting to keep calm, to let happen what was to happen, only, there was protest as well, and she was afraid of it. "All packed?" she asked lightly.

He nodded his head, then smiled, for he realized that none of this was easy for her, in fact, her bravery, as he chose to call it, made him feel admiration. She was holding up beautifully, and for a woman who held on to everything tightly, he understood the strain she must be under. "Mona," he began reticently. "I know none of the past few years has been easy for you, I mean living with me in such a state most of the time, but I want you to know that I have always wanted you to be happy. To know that I could not bring you the happiness you deserve has always been a painful fact which I have often had to face. I know how much you want happiness. I know what it means to you. But the more I think about what I am doing now, the more certain I am it's the only answer for me. *My* only chance for being happy too."

Why does he have to say anything now? Hasn't he said enough for one evening? "I do think you are being very selfish," she said quickly. "But then, Michael, I think you always have been selfish."

A half smile formed on his lips. "The one thing I have found out in the last few weeks, Mona, is that to have personal happiness you must be selfish. Happiness is a very personal state of mind."

But what about my happiness? she wanted to scream at him. What about mine? But she had acquired a strange sort of pride suddenly. And anyway, she knew that he would be back in a week. "Michael," she said carefully. "What happens if you find that the monastery doesn't have what you're searching for?"

"Right now I don't know the answer to that, Mona," he replied honestly. "But I should think that if God fails me or I fail God you certainly wouldn't want me back here. After all, my coming back would make you feel like you were a second choice."

"Second choice?" she cried out. It's God that's second choice, she wanted to say, but she was smart enough to realize that she must weigh her words carefully here. She must not make him feel that she was waiting for him to return. But she was never too good at handling complex, delicate situations. Somehow she had to blurt out what she thought or felt. She could not contain subterfuge too well. Above all else, she must not become spiteful and full of petty revenge. She usually got the worst of it. "That's up to you, Michael," she said finally. There, that was better.

She had come a long way since the day she broke her doll.

She was eight. Someone had given her a doll with a china head. The hair was painted black with long curls. The porcelain cheeks were delicate with a reddish tinge. The eyes were painted charmingly and she was such a beautiful doll. But one day, because she was furious at her mother about something, she picked up the doll, knowing full well that what she was about to do could never be undone, and hurled it full of anger against the wall. The china head had cracked apart like a nut shell split with a hammer. The limp doll fell to the floor with pieces of chipped and shattered glass. She could recall perfectly how she stood there, and said over and over again, "I don't care. I don't care." Yet, later that night, because she could not sleep, she had gotten up, and with reverent fingers, she picked up the doll and one by one she found the pieces of the head and cupped them in her trembling fingers. Tears streamed down her cheeks.

Somehow she had brought unhappiness on herself through revenge. She had meant to hurt her mother but she had only hurt herself. She did not want to do the same thing now, with Michael. "What are you going to do about Anna Martin?" she asked. "You know that she is very much in love with you. Don't you feel any responsibility to her?"

"Of course I do," he admitted. "But I'm not responsible for her feelings towards me. I did nothing to encourage it."

No, she thought to herself angrily. You didn't do anything to encourage it. You took her out to lunch, sent her a present. Really, his conceit was too much. "Maybe you're doing the right thing after all," she said. "I mean about going into a monastery. You won't be able to do as much harm there."

"Harm?" he asked.

"Let's forget it," she said quickly.

"I want to know what you meant by that." They both stood up at the same time, facing each other.

She was losing control of herself and she knew it. She could feel resentment rising rapidly. "I mean," she said sharply, "that you've always been thinking of yourself. You never did give a damn about what happened to me or the children."

"That's not true," he cut in. "I've always cared about what happened to you but I couldn't do anything about it. If I didn't know *what* could make me happy, how could I make *you* happy?"

"Couldn't you sacrifice yourself a little?"

"Sacrifice?" he exclaimed. "Well, if you'd like to know, I've sacrificed myself enough. I'm through sacrificing. Everything here has been a sacrifice. You, the children, this house, they're all monuments to me, and I've been buried under them too long."

"Get out of here," she cried out furiously. "Get your old bag and get out."

Neither one of them moved. Then he said, "We're both acting pretty ridiculous."

She was trembling. "Look," she said tensely. "There's not much point in our going on like this now, is there? I mean, not until you've been to a monastery. Not until you know for certain what you want to do. I've had quite a day. I'm going up to bed." She tried giving him an understanding smile. After all, they were still married. Wasn't she one of his monuments? "Good night," she said hesitantly.

He nodded his head. His eyes followed her as she walked across the room and disappeared up the stairs. He could hear her heels on the floor above. He sat down, exhausted. He was alone for the first time that day. Or was he?

He sensed that now the old Michael Humphrey had just about been completely replaced with the new one, the wise one, the gentle one, and that other, unhappy, confused, tormented Michael Humphrey had completely disappeared, or almost, had vanished like smoke into the air. And with the old one went his past, his way of life that he had been living up until now. There was little left. He was a different person all together. Life had been, up until today, one long, tedious wrestle with an invisible adversary. He was not certain if he was resurrecting himself or burying himself. Or were there many selves? Had he simply buried one, and brought up another into light? Could there still be another ready to replace this one? And on and on.

If I just knew how to pray, he thought. I've never been able to ask for anything. And if there was a God, how did one find Him? *What* was the key? *Where* was the door? *Who* found whom? He did not know but he was positive that the direction he was going in was the right one for him. But just suppose it was a mistake. What would he do then? Where would he go? Where does one go after God? He bowed his head. Oh, God, please show me how to pray. Please. I want to learn.

* * *

Upstairs, Mona was wiping makeup from her face. Even though her hands still trembled, there was an odd sort of smile on her lips. Second choice, she was thinking. She had been going over the events of the entire day in her mind, and they all added up to one answer. He would never last. This was a whim, a digression. He needed a vacation. This was his. After all, she was still married to him. She had legal rights if nothing else. Second choice, she thought again with amusement. That may be, but he was her one and only choice. She had only to wait – she had only to be patient. She had invested too much of her time, too much of her youth, too much of her self in his to let him go that easily. Even God couldn't take him away from her with out a fight. He was too weak. Couldn't *God* see that? He'd never stand up under it. Poor Michael! But he'd be back. There was no doubt of it in her mind.

Chapter Twenty-Two

The next morning, Mrs. Ross sat alone at the breakfast table. The sunlight filtered through two large windows in the dining room touching the silver on the table with quick, white sparks. Mary had thoughtfully arranged a centerpiece of jonquils but Mrs. Ross had not noticed. Her face was crinkly and, for once, badly powdered. Even her immaculate hair was slightly disarranged. She, herself, had hardly slept a wink. If she had gone over the events of the afternoon once before, she had done it at least four times more. First, that dreadfully smug woman deliberately out to hurt Anna, and then that pathetic man with those sad yellow roses in his hand. I never want to go through another day like that one, she confided in herself. But most of all, what caused her more suffering than all the rest was to watch the liveliness, the quick smiles, the out- and outright happiness fade from Anna's face, like a rose brought in too quickly to a hot room. The color fades instantaneously while the petals fall lifelessly to the floor. And then, what was she to write to her daughter, Martha? How was she able to tell her? Exactly what should she let her know? She would certainly have to prepare her. Anna could never bear this blow alone.

Mary came in with some hot coffee. Mrs. Ross watched her quietly, but felt no need whatever to speak. Then, what she had been waiting for occurred. There were footsteps on the stairs. Mary looked anxiously down at Mrs. Ross.

"Is she all right this morning, Mrs. Ross?" Mary whispered.

"I don't know," replied Mrs. Ross. "She went to bed early

last night. I never heard a sound after that." She looked out in the hallway as Anna approached. "My dear, we were going to let you sleep as late as you wanted." She smiled nervously at her granddaughter.

Anna hesitated in the doorway, because she could tell from the concern on both of the women's faces that they had been discussing her. "I wanted to get up early," she replied, walking towards her grandmother. "There's an awful lot of things that I want to do." She kissed her gently on the cheek, then sat down.

Mrs. Ross glanced significantly across at Mary. "Really," she said, trying not to sound too inquisitive. "What kind of things?"

Anna took a swallow from her orange juice. She put the glass down then looked over at Mrs. Ross. "I'm going home today."

There was a respectful silence.

"I'll scramble you some eggs, Miss Anna," said Mary, then she hurriedly headed for the kitchen.

Mrs. Ross took a long swallow of coffee. "What made you come to this decision?" She put her cup down carefully.

Anna picked up her orange juice again. "I stayed up most all night. I guess it must have been around four when I finally closed my eyes. I did a lot of thinking."

"And your thinking brought you to this decision to leave?" smiled Mrs. Ross helpfully.

"Yes," Anna nodded her head. "It did."

"Anna," said Mrs. Ross, reaching out for her hand. "I don't mean to pry or want to offer you advice where it isn't needed, but please don't let what happened to you yesterday prejudice you against life. Some people would, you know. They think that because one thing turns out badly everything else will."

"One thing?" remarked Anna. "This makes two things now."

"My dear, please be patient," begged her grandmother.

"Everything will come. You'll see."

"I'm not really impatient," said Anna with a smile. "In fact, I've learned a great deal about myself and about life from both of these apparent failures of mine."

"That's the only way to take life," insisted Mrs. Ross. "One can't be safe continually. One must dip into life, gradually, if possible, but if not, one must plunge sooner or later into the midst of it or one never learns anything. Just regrets," she added nostalgically.

"Well," said Anna with a certain amount of humor in her voice. "I'll have had two plunges. Now, maybe I'll try the dips."

"Oh, you are getting cynical," exclaimed Mrs. Ross. "It frightens me to hear you speak like that."

Anna laughed softly. "Not really cynical," she explained. "Maybe just a little tired and irritable."

"That's the same thing," said Mrs. Ross.

Anna glanced in her direction. "Poor Grandmother! I have been such a problem to you in these past few weeks. Won't you be pleased to have me go?"

"Don't talk nonsense," chided Mrs. Ross. "Now tell me, what have you learned about yourself overnight? What wonderful discovery was it that kept you awake until dawn?"

Anna thought a moment, trying to arrange her words carefully, for she *had* learned something, even though in her mind what she had learned was still vague, vague yet pronounced like the outline of trees just before dawn strips them of their shadows, bringing them into sharp relief, exposing them finally as trees, leafed and sturdy. "I'm not certain if what I say will make too much sense, but as I see it, there are different types of love in this world but you can divide them into two main categories. The love for God and the love for man. If you want to give yourself completely to something, like Michael does, then God would be the answer. But if you just don't happen to feel that way, then I think you turn to human beings. After all, in the end, you can only have a perfect love if the object is perfection. No human beings are perfect. Therefore—"

"Therefore," interrupted Mrs. Ross, "all human love would be imperfect."

"Exactly," exclaimed Anna. "That's why in this country, for instance, there is so much falseness, so much confusion about love. In the movies they keep making out that what they are after is perfect love, only what they get is just human affection in the end. It takes a great deal of strength to choose God. You put on yourself so many more obligations. I just wasn't able to hold up under them," she admitted reticently. "I only hope that Michael can."

"I guess then the great problem is not to get them mixed up," suggested Mrs. Ross, remembering the relationship with her deceased husband. She had made very certain not to mix up that relationship.

"Yes," said Anna, looking down at the table cloth. "That's the great problem. I got them mixed up. I was demanding from Christ what I really wanted from a human being. I suppose Michael was demanding only what God could satisfy. Foolishly enough, I thought it was me he was after."

"Well, my dear," said Mrs. Ross solemnly. "Then you have learned a great deal."

"Yes," smiled Anna sadly, "I have."

Mary came in with the rest of Anna's breakfast. "Them eggs is fresh this morning," she remarked.

After Mary went back into the kitchen, Mrs. Ross said, "Why are you going home today?"

"Don't you see, Grandmother," said Anna, buttering a piece of toast. "I can go home now. I'm not afraid to face the family. I know now that I didn't have that perfect love that was necessary to give God. All I had to offer was human love."

"But doesn't that disappoint you?" asked Mrs. Ross. "I mean, that you weren't able to give perfect love?"

Anna shook her head. "Not in the least. There's no point in my trying to give something I'm not capable of giving. If I can find someone who wants just what human love has to offer, respect, companionship, affection, concern; then I'm sure I could make him very happy. But I haven't got the other in me."

"I see," said Mrs. Ross. Indeed, she thought proudly, Anna was certainly right. Render to Caesar the things that are Caesar's and to God the things that are God's. But of course that was why so many people were miserable with their lives. They keep confusing the perfect with the imperfect. Lovers kept insisting that the other be perfection. How much more wonderful imperfections was then perfection? She knew which side she was on. When you're faced with perfection all your inadequacies turned out to be faults, but once you acknowledged imperfection you had so much more room to move about in, so much more to strive for, to hope for. "Anna dear, you simply amaze me," she cried out. "And this does explain why poor Mr. Humphrey wants to stay in a monastery for a time."

"Yes," she said softly, "that's why he's going. He senses that God is the answer to his problem. Absolute perfection. I only hope he finds what he's searching for. If he's strong enough and patient enough, he may find it."

"But if he doesn't, what then?"

"I don't know," she replied. The one thing that she regretted most was that she had not wished him well. Now she knew what a strain he must have been under yesterday.

"What about his wife?" asked Mrs. Ross. "Surely, if she came over here like she did yesterday, she would never let him go that easily."

"No," admitted Anna. "She would never let him go that easily."

"Then you think she expects him to fail?" wondered Mrs. Ross.

"Yes," said Anna softly. "That's exactly what she expects him to do."

"Poor Mr. Humphrey," exclaimed Mrs. Ross. Affectionately she reached across to pat her granddaughter's hand. "Would you like some more coffee?"

"Please." Then Anna told her she was going to pack as soon as she finished eating. "I'll call Mother and tell her I'm coming on the afternoon train."

"You do that, my dear," said Mrs. Ross. "I'm sure that she will be very glad to hear your voice again."

Just before Anna left to go upstairs she stood up, put her arms around her grandmother and hugged her tightly. "I'm so glad that I was here with you.... I mean to have you to go through this experience with me. No one else would have ever understood and been as patient as you've been."

"Well, my dear," smiled Mrs. Ross. "That's due to years and years of practicing my own kind of imperfect love. I'm only pleased that you needed me."

After Anna had left the dining room, Mrs. Ross sat there pensively alone for quite some time. The sun had moved up over the tops of the houses so that the rays disappeared from the table. Shadows had entered now. The silver was just silver. The dishes were just dishes. No magic sparkle from the sunlight. No.... But she stopped. There in the center of the table were the jonquils. Freshly yellow and fragrant. She had not arranged them nor had she placed them there. But the thoughtfulness, which she was certain was Mary's, suddenly seemed to make all the difference in the world to her. After all, she said to herself, this too, is an expression of love, the desire to please. And what a dreary place this world would be without it. What bareness would exist. What fearful loneliness. When Mrs. Ross finally stood up, she made her way directly to the kitchen. Mary was eating her breakfast.

"Is everything all right, Mrs. Ross?' she asked kindly, putting down her coffee cup.

"Everything's find, Mary," replied Mrs. Ross warmly. "And thank you, Mary, for putting the jonquils on the table this morning. They're lovely."

Mary beamed with pleasure. Mrs. Ross realized in that instant that to love someone *was* a very great thing but to be able to acknowledge that love was *even* greater.

Chapter Twenty-Three

Beatrice Drake saw him by accident. She opened the front door to pick up the morning paper, which the Senator had forgotten to bring inside. There was Michael Humphrey walking down the street with a suitcase in his hand. He stopped a cab, got in and drove away. My God, thought Bea, he's left her. She hurriedly picked up the newspaper, rushed inside and picked up the phone. She dialed feverishly.

"Darling," she asked casually, "are you busy? I thought I'd drop over for a spot of coffee."

A hesitant, "All right."

"I'll just stay for a few minutes. I know you must have a lot to do."

"Just for a few minutes," came Mona's toneless reply.

She sounded like she's been crying, thought Bea as she stepped out of her house and into the one next door.

She did not bother to knock. But when she walked inside and saw Mona come running out of the kitchen, she realized that she had hoped it would be Michael.

Mona blushed. "I could hear you coming," she explained. "I thought maybe the door might be locked."

Her eyes looked dreadful, Bea noticed.

"It's black coffee for you, isn't it, Bea?" she asked as she went back into the kitchen.

"Yes, dear," Bea glanced exploringly around the room for any clues that might tell her what had occurred. There was no broken glass anywhere. The pillows on the sofa were all in place. "Mona dear," called Bea. "Wasn't that Michael I saw leaving here just a few minutes ago with a suitcase?" Silence in the kitchen. "Has he gone on a trip?" Still more silence. "Did you hear me, Mona dear?"

"Yes," said Mona, bringing in the coffee on a tray. "I heard you. And that was Michael you saw. And he *is* going on a trip."

Mona straightened up. Bea would never give her any peace. "Bea," she began. "We've lived here now for eight years and you've been a wonderful neighbor. I know you're not trying to pry into our affairs. You're genuinely interested. But this time, rather than evade your questions, I'm going to ask you not to ask me any."

"You mean it's that serious," asked Bea, her eyes wide open with curiosity.

"No," she replied angrily. "I don't mean it's that serious."

"All right, darling," said Bea, patting her hand affectionately. "I won't ask another question. Let's talk about something else, shall we?"

But, thought Mona tiredly, what else was there to talk about? She hadn't slept a wink the whole night long. She exerted the most rigid control over her behavior because she wanted more than anything to crawl into his bed, to hold on to him, to have him hold on to her, but she felt defeated.

In more ways than one he was right about being second choice. It did leave her in a most unfair position, but hadn't she been in that position most of her married life? Then when he had gotten up, showered and gone downstairs for breakfast, all without saying a word to her, she had felt more left out than ever before.

But it was the suitcase sitting down in the foyer that struck the most destructive blow. There it sat, black and alien. All it meant to her was that he was going away on a trip, a voyage somewhere, and he was leaving her behind. Her greatest fear had been realized. She was being abandoned. He had been very pleasant at breakfast, for he had made breakfast for all of them. When the children had come down he was more than considerate, telling them that he was going away for a few days. They believed him. Thank God he hadn't left that problem up to her. But once the children had gone outside, they both found it difficult to speak. She drank her coffee mechanically. He did the same. Then suddenly he stood up.

"Thank you, Mona, for being as considerate as you have been," he said politely. "I think maybe now you've got a good chance to find the happiness you've been hunting for."

"The happiness that I've been hunting for?" She looked up inquiringly at him.

"Yes," he said gently. "You've been looking for it in me, only it wasn't there. Now maybe this time—"

"But I don't want another time," she cried out indignantly. "I only want this time."

"But *this* time is over," he said quietly. "It's run its course. It's ended. Can't you see that? The end is always in the beginning of everything. And if you're honest, you'll admit it."

"Well, I'm not honest," she had said. "And I don't want to be. I just want you."

Then he looked at her tenderly. "Mona," he said full of embarrassment. "I don't know how to pray yet, but when I do, I'll pray every day that you find that happiness."

"Oh, don't be an ass!" she had flung back at him. "Really, Michael, religion does not become you. It doesn't fit in with your personality."

"I hope to *make* it fit in," he replied, walking over to pick up his suitcase.

"Oh please," she had called out tearfully. "Aren't you even going to kiss me good-bye?"

He hesitated. "Of course."

But the condescending way he had said it infuriated her. "Never mind," she had said. She refused to get up from the table to see him leave. She had sat there sipping her coffee. He waited. Then finally he had said good-bye. She never turned her head. The door opened and closed. Silence walked in. Still she sat there. In her hands the cup trembled. But she refused to give in to her feelings of panic. He'll come back. That's all there is to this. Sheer nonsense. He'll come back to me. He hasn't got the strength to stay away.

Then the phone rang. She answered it. Bea was on the line. Now here they sat, one across from the other.

"Bea," she said finally, in a dull, toneless voice. "Michael will be back. I know he will."

So, thought Mrs. Drake, it's true. He has left her. "Of course he'll be back," she said soothingly. "Now why don't you go upstairs, take a nice shower, then we'll go downtown and do some nice shopping together."

"Shopping?" Mona repeated. She tried to smile. "Yes, maybe I should get out of the house. Maybe that would help a little."

"Shopping for a woman helps a lot of things," said Beatrice humorously.

And they did shop. They went from Neiman's to Saks, Mona bought five pairs of shoes and two hats more than she needed. Beatrice had two Manhattans, while Mona carefully sipped one. Beatrice was in the midst of telling about the time a millionaire from Dallas had sent up a plane especially so they could come to an evening party when Mona reached out, full of panic, and clutched onto Bea's hand. With obvious fear in her eyes she asked, "He *will* come back to me, won't he? He will? He must!" Then suddenly she began to cry.

"That's right, dear," said Bea solicitously, "Cry it out. My motto has always been that you can't get your self-respect back unless you have humiliated yourself with tears." She reached out and stopped a waitress. "Two more Manhattans, dear." She turned back to Mona. "And believe me, the best way to get results is have another drink. Manhattans and tears go beautifully together."

Chapter Twenty-Four

In the middle of the cloister, there was a rectangular garden centered with a rectangular fountain. For the past three afternoons Michael Humphrey had made it a habit of walking there, back and forth, thinking, trying to recall various happenings in his life, hoping to understand what they meant to him. In and out of his memory went, poking here, prodding there, hunting for that particular one that would uncover his unconscious search for God. That particular one was difficult to find. Yet, he knew it was there, shadowy, but certainly there, like the sun behind clouds at midday.

Michael had discovered the garden quite by accident because the monks very seldom had time to stroll there. They were busy from sunup to sundown. They were either praying or teaching. In the beginning he had felt very embarrassed among them, an awkwardness that was similar to the time he had been brought into a new classroom as a new pupil. Yet, as the hours passed, and he became used to the quiet, the distance disappeared. He ate separately from them but at the same table. He watched them furtively and he knew they were watching him with interest. They, consequently, became more human, more real. Even though they were, as yet, unable to speak to each other, for he was kept apart, he knew they were aware of his presence as much as he was of theirs.

During the day he tried reading various religious books that had been placed surreptitiously next to his bed, but miracles, stigmatas and other religious phenomena were too far advanced for him to comprehend. He was still struggling with his rudimentary willingness to believe. Several times he had gone alone into the chapel, hoping that some religious fervor would seize him, as the books he had looked at intimated could happen. To the special God-chosen few, of course. He had tried to pray unselfconsciously but he was inevitably aware of a tincture of insincerity in his praying. Something was wrong. At night he would talk to Father Gregory at great length. Father Gregory had sensible answers for most of his doubts.

"Doesn't Jesus say somewhere that the Kingdom of God is within you?" Michael had asked the night before.

"Oh, yes," replied the monk.

"But how do you find that Kingdom?" asked Michael exasperated by the confusion. "Where do you discover the key?"

Father Gregory smiled tolerantly. "You find it, of course, through the Catholic Church."

Always that same solution. Always the Catholic Church. But what Michael did not like about this solution was that the Catholic Church handed you not *one* key, but an entire *ring* of them, doctrines and prohibitions for every occasion. In fact, they not only handed you the keys but they gave you the lock and the door with it.

So each afternoon he went by himself in the quiet garden to find the key. He noticed that the tulips were up and the hyacinth were in full bloom. He thought fleetingly of his own garden back in Georgetown. He thought of Mona, of Anna, of his children. But they all belonged to another world now. They were like lingering shadows that were all but faded. At night, however, when the sacred quietness had descended in the cloister, and he pictured each monk in each of the different, row upon row of cells, lying on his back, or perhaps even kneeling by his bed, he would recall a smile, a gesture, a tone of voice from someone he had known, and he would be touched with an undignified restlessness. But what embarrassed him more than all the rest was that each night he would be plunged back into consciousness by a repetitive nightmare he was having. Even though the images vanished before his eyes opened, the tail end of a scream tingled in his ears. That child's mother again.

Back and forth he walked on the grass. Birds chatted nervously. There was a small cherry tree over to one side of the pool. On the first afternoon he had been there he noticed a mother robin was busily making herself a nest. The tree was not a very high one. Even at the time he wondered why she had chosen such a dangerous location. There were many higher trees around. Today, she had just about finished the shaping of it, for he noticed her moving energetically about, rounding it out against the shape of her plump body. The feverish haste of motherhood. There was a bench over against the wall. He went over, sat down, closed his eyes and let the warmth from the sun heat his face and hands. There was a winter chill still lingering inside the cloister, which had penetrated into his body. The sun counteracted this chill. He took a small black prayer book out of his pocket.

At that moment he heard a snapping sound. Looking up he saw a gray, lean cat making its stealthy way across the grass towards the tree where the robin was still busily finishing up her nest. Had the cat seen the bird? Michael was afraid to move. The cat slowed down. No doubt of it. The cat stopped to watch the feathery movement in the nest. Evidently the bird was too intent to notice the danger that waited below. Then quick as a flash, the cat sprung up the tree like a young, healthy leopard, and before he could do anything to stop it, the cat was up at the nest. The bird gave a shrill cry of alarm, its wings beat frantically against her assailant. She had got up out of the nest halfway, but the cat struck out with a deadly claw.

Michael sprang towards the tree, shouting angrily at the cat.

For a second, the cat stopped to look at the intruder while the bird beat furiously against its face with a wing. The cat struck again, and bit furiously into the bird's body. Michael hit up at the cat with the prayer book, knocking it halfway down the limb. The cat clung with one paw to the trunk while the bird teetered on the edge of the nest, then plunged down into the shrubbery. Both Michael and the cat made a dive for it. Michael hurled the black book at the cat's head as hard as he could. The cat made a sound like a baby doll that had been squeezed too tight. It gave one last long lingering look at the crippled bird, then scurried resentfully away.

The bird's right wing was splayed out like a fan that had been forced open too far, exposing the polished quills. There were bright red beads glistening on the feathers. As he reached over to touch the bird, its body quivered, its yellow eyes looked wildly into his, its beak opened and shut, making a whiney sound. Gently he slid his hand underneath its trembling body. He could feel the heartbeats drumming a hundred a minute. The left wing was intact but the right one hung down helplessly over his hand, lifeless yet quivering.

Once he had crawled out of the shrubbery and into the sunlight, he held the bird up for closer inspection. She was maternally nervous. She apparently knew that with a broken wing she was doomed. Majestically she allowed herself to be held in his hand now, but the tattered, useless wing hung worthlessly downward, and as he reached out to lift it up carefully, the robin pecked viciously at his fingers. This time, when he glanced into the bird's eyes, he noticed that the wild, frantic look had gone, being replaced with a look of sorrow, of utter futility, an expression that he was suddenly aware of having seen recently. Once again, with striking force, he remembered the look in the mother's eyes as she held out her arms to receive her newly killed son. Only this time with this dreadful recollection came the same tugging sensation, the same nagging unexplained reaction that he had felt that day. His mouth opened and closed automatically. He was trying to utter, 'Forgive me.... Please forgive me,' like the unfortunate driver had. What did his reaction mean? Why had he been so completely overwhelmed emotionally? This time, however, the sensation he was feeling was not as powerful as it had been that day on the Memorial Bridge. The shock of witnessing death was removed. He was able to dig into the midst of it, and with a startled recognition he realized that the overwhelming emotion that he had felt that day was *compassion*. He recognized it now. And with this feeling of compassion came an actual awareness, an actual sense of the nearness of God. So compassion was the key then. The key he had been searching for. One found God through compassion. "Forgive me...." he said aloud, to himself for not realizing, to God for not seeing. "Forgive me," for the years he had squandered, to the people he had ignored, to the world he had not experienced.

The robin moved restlessly in his hand. There were stains of blood across his fingers. "Don't worry," he smiled at the bird. "I'll take care of you. I'll heal your wing. Don't be afraid." A drop of compassion had fallen into his soul, shattering his very foundations. What joy! What comfort to know it could be increased.

He glanced up suddenly at the garden around him, at the trees fisted with blossoms, at the vines quivering with new leaves. A heaviness was lifted in that instant. He had found the key at last. The world was no longer separated from him, they were together, one a part of the other. For the world and all of life was a manifestation of God's compassion. Now, Michael Humphrey could become a part of compassion, too. He had found the key to that Kingdom inside himself, that last, last hiding place of God. He cupped the bird protectively against his chest, then knelt humbly on the grass. He started to look heavenward, then remembered God was no longer in His

Heaven. He was down on the earth now, inside, waiting, and oh, what a relief it was for Michael to know, *He* was compassionate.

*